PRAISE FOR VIOLATION HIVE

"An imagination like no other, *Violation Hive* is part Barker, part Lovecraft but 100% Steele. A conjurer of the most immersive new worlds you'll ever read, this is what Ridley Scott dreams about."

— STEVE STRED, AUTHOR OF *RITUAL*

"Brian Fatah Steele's *Violation Hive* features an array of cosmic horrors culled from down your street as well as all the way out to deepest space. In reading these tales, I couldn't wait to turn the page to see what horrors awaited, and believe me, these are creepy, chaotic horrors infused with grotesque imagery, all dished out with genuinely enthusiastic glee, as if Steele is having fun, which is infectious. As a reader, I always wanted more!"

— JOHN CLAUDE SMITH, AUTHOR OF *OCCASIONAL BEASTS: TALES* AND THE BRAM STOKER AWARD FINALIST FIRST NOVEL, *RIDING THE CENTIPEDE*

"*Violation Hive* is cosmic horror done right. From the first story, in which a down-on-his-luck graphic designer discovers a sarcophagus at a nearby building site, to later science fiction journeys into the Deeper Black, Brian Fatah Steele describes encounters with things beyond our comprehension and universe with unfaltering courage and psychological insight. His characters are grounded and human, his prose is stylistic but controlled, and his mythos is at once Lovecraftian and entirely his own. Several stories in this collection will stay with me forever."

— JOSEPH SALE, AUTHOR OF THE BLACK GATE TRILOGY

"With *Violation Hive,* Brian Fatah Steele brings the most otherworldly horrors down to earth where they can wreak the most havoc. This collection had me fearing my neighbors more than any infinite beyond."

— SONORA TAYLOR, AWARD-WINNING AUTHOR OF *LITTLE PARANOIAS: STORIES.*

"Brian Fatah Steele writes like a madman who is part wizard, part robot. *Violation Hive* will set your mind on a weird and cosmic roller coaster, blending worlds of horror and sci-fi into one screaming unit of awesome! Imaginative, lucid stuff!"

— JOE ZITO, AUTHOR OF *NOW COMES THE DARKNESS*

"Brian Fatah Steele, master of the tender everyday ripped asunder, takes us on a wild ride through his phantasmagoric universe with *Violation Hive*. From the classic sci-fi and horror setups we all love to read, to original and thought-provoking scenarios, the only guarantee with these stories is that the unexpected and frightening will lurk around every corner."

— BP GREGORY, AUTHOR OF FLORA & JIM

"Take a pinch of horror, sprinkle in a generous helping of sci-fi, then add a bit of deliciously weird, and you've got *Violation Hive*. No matter what you're into, this collection is a disturbingly great read."

— RENEE MILLER, AUTHOR OF STRANDED

"*Violation Hive* is Steele's most gut-wrenching, mind-bending collection of tales to date. It highlights his uncanny ability to put a modern, macabre spin on cosmic horror in a variety of genres, and should be an essential addition to any speculative fiction fans' library."

— JEREMY HEPLER, BRAM STOKER
NOMINATED AUTHOR OF THE BOULEVARD
MONSTER

"Brian Fatah Steele's new collection, *Violation Hive* is a world all of its own. It's full of futuristic and post-apocalyptic cosmic horror coated in a layer of extraterrestrial slime, one of its many tentacles rooted in ancient rituals and another buried deep enough under Appalachia to keep me feeling grounded but never at ease."

— MIRANDA CRITES, KENDALL REVIEWS

VIOLATION HIVE

AND OTHER STORIES

BRIAN FATAH STEELE

What do you believe in? Do your beliefs empower you or make you fearful? Some walk alone as others find fellowship, all seeking answers. Zealots, devoid of doubt, proclaim their versions of the truth. Ideas are contagious, and in the dark, the worst ideas can consume us.

Ten tales of cosmic horror from the author of CELESTIAL SEEPAGE and HUNGRY RAIN. From a neighborhood ravaged by a cult worshipping a mutagenic plague, to passengers racing across a dystopian wasteland. A group of girls discovering something ancient in an old barn, to a man stumbling into a mirror world populated by lunatics. A secret base engaged in a disastrous experiment, to a space station infected by an alien intelligence.

These and more inside, ready to make you question everything.

CONTENTS

Other Books By Brian Fatah Steele xiii

Acknowledgments xv

1. VIOLATION HIVE I
2. I SEE YOU BETWEEN THE STARS 33
3. BLIGHT ON YOUR TONGUE 47
4. ALWAYS FACE DIRECTLY INTO RUIN 70
5. FUTURE EXPRESSIONS 81
6. YOUR ACOLYTE EYES 102
7. GLIMPSE OF DULL KNIVES 118
8. PALE REMAINS OF ROYALTY 130
9. A DIRGE EVERENDING 142
10. OUROBOROS MORNING 168

About the Author 175

For my brother, Quintin…

ACKNOWLEDGMENTS

Quarantine began in Ohio on March 25th. That was the day I began working on a new book. On December 31st, I finished the last short story for this collection. In that time, I wrote two novels, a collection, and started Dimensionaut Media to make pre-made art for book covers. Sure, Quarantine drove me further down the path of insanity, but I was damn productive.

I have to confess, about three or four of these short stories were already done when I started this project. As I was hammering out ideas for more tales, a kind of theme started to take shape. Maybe it was due to the political atmosphere at the time, but everything kept coming back to the idea of belief. I decided to lean into that in different ways, while still keeping focused on fun explorations into cosmic horror. Through this, I was able to tell a few stories I'd had lingering in my skull for years.

Short story writing is different than novels for me, so my music was all over the place. I listened to a lot of Lana Del Rey and Bring Me The Horizon, Lorde and Puscifer, Halsey and TK. This is what you ended up with.

This community is awesome, and I always appreciate all the support it gives me. Thanks to Armand Rosamilia, Don

Noble, Steve Stred, Pete Kahle, Glenn Rolfe, Tim Meyer, Michelle Garza, Melissa Lason, Joe Zito, Somer Canon, Salome Jones, BP Gregory, Maurice Broaddus, Sonora Taylor, Chuck Buda, John Claude Smith, Kyle Lybeck, and CW Hawes. You guys have all made screaming into the void a bit more bearable, even if you didn't know it. This book is only readable thanks to the editing and formatting of Joseph Sale.

Gotta thank some people around me, too. Jonathan and Annie Joyce, Joe Shaffer, Dan and Brittany Weymouth, Kendell Gibson, Sierra Jones, Tyler Vetter, along with my brothers Nathan, Jordan, Quintin, and my sister-in-laws. Always the shout out to my parents, as well.

Quintin, you wanted short stories. Here are your damn short stories…

❦   I   ❦

VIOLATION HIVE

It sounded like the world was ending.

Calvin woke up swearing, his cat bolting from the corner of the bed. The cacophony shook his bedroom as he looked around and gritted his teeth. A quick glance at the clock at the end table told him it was a quarter to nine in the morning. Staggering out of the sheets, he made his way to the window and pulled back the curtains.

A construction crew had assembled next door, materialized at some point earlier that morning. They were in the process of tearing down the abandoned house next door. Jesus fuck.

Yanking on a pair of sweat pants and his robe, Calvin made his way downstairs. He tried to pet Zeus, but there was another boom from outside. The cat fled behind the television, his normal hiding spot during thunderstorms. Waking Calvin up was one thing, but scaring his cat officially pissed him off.

Marching outside, he starting yelling at the construction crew, demanding to see their foreman. In no time at all, a short man with thick arms and wide smile ambled up to him. He introduced himself and said the company had been trying to contact Calvin, explaining some of the details.

Calvin didn't really pay attention. Still half asleep, he pieced together that the neighboring house was another one of the abandoned properties in town, seized by the city. It had been deemed condemned, so slated for demolition. This was the sixteenth building in the last two months. Vetter, Ohio was on a steady decline, no matter how many houses got torn down.

As the foreman went into the explanation for the second time, Calvin realized this was all pointless. He would simply have to deal with it. Told they would be done by Friday afternoon, it took him a moment to remember what day it was. Wednesday. He supposed he could live with the noise for a few days.

Grumbling, he went back inside to check on his cat.

THE WHOLE BLOCK Calvin lived on sat in the south side of Vetter, what some still desperately wanted to call the Historical District. All the houses were over a century old and also falling apart. No one with money lived here, or had the money to properly fix them up. Some sections were rife with crime, a notorious traphouse only a block away filled with heroin users. Residents tried the best they could, and there were always whispers of gentrification, but nothing ever developed.

The house that was being demolished sat at the end of the block, with Calvin next door in a small brick home. There were a few other homes occupied on the block, but not many. The only neighbors he ever interacted with were Benny and Grace across the street. They had all known each other for years, reconnecting in their mid-thirties when the couple had moved after getting married four years ago.

Calvin watched Benny pull up, right on time.

Calvin stepped off his porch and strolled over with two

cups of coffee. He had to grin as he watched Benny climb out of the car and gape at the wreckage across from him.

"Did you get angry and punch the house?" he asked.

"No, but all the noise did wake me up."

"Oh, I'm sure you were thrilled with that."

Calvin handed him the coffee. "There was swearing."

"Thanks," he said, taking the coffee. "You know the way to my heart."

They went up on Benny's porch, and both lit up cigarettes. Benny worked as an engineer at a car manufacturing plant, and he alone could have afforded a much nicer house without Grace's income. She was a Director of Nursing and made as much as him. Calvin wasn't entirely sure what they were doing living here.

"You think they're going to hit the house on the other side of you?" asked Benny.

Calvin peered at it. It was a small redbrick structure that looked almost identical to his. An elderly couple had lived there for decades up until just six months ago, when the wife died and the husband went into a nursing home. Their children lived across the country.

"I doubt it. That place is still in decent shape. It could easily sell, or be used as a rental property."

Benny snorted. "As long as we don't have any squatters migrating in. I've been keeping an eye on the place."

"Same here."

Vetter was overrun with drugs and a lack of opportunities. No local jobs, failing health care system, virtually non-existent police force. The school board prioritized sports over education because it brought in money. Every year more citizens left and the town got a little worse.

"How's the job hunt going?" Benny asked.

Calvin groaned. "It's going, not sure where though."

As a graphic designer, Calvin had worked for years with a studio out of Pittsburgh. When Covid hit, it hadn't been that big of a deal for all of them to go remote instead of working from offices. Unfortunately, when the yearly budget review came, the company realized it could save even more money, and cut half its staff. Calvin had been getting by doing freelance work, but eventually he would need a permanent gig, especially something that gave him benefits.

Benny had offered to lend him money, but Calvin didn't think he was there yet. Still, it was nice to know he had a friend like that in his corner. The two of them had spent many nights sitting on the porch, drinking coffee, chain smoking, and complaining.

An hour later, Grace came home with eighties pop music announcing her arrival. Where Benny was grumpy, she was whimsical. Unbelievably tall and slender, with anime-like eyes, she popped out of the car and pointed over at the debris.

"The fuck happened there?"

"Tornado," Calvin and Benny said in unison, the story they had agreed upon.

"Shut up, no it wasn't. You're both lying to me again. I can see the bulldozer."

"Baby, if you can see the bulldozer, why are you asking the question?"

"You're not getting any tacos now."

Unbeknownst to Calvin, Benny had texted his wife and she had brought food for him, too. He thanked them both, and dug in. As they ate, they discussed the house across the street and what that could mean for the neighborhood. Grace had some wild speculations, and Benny only foresaw doom.

Finishing up, Grace stood. "I wanna inspect it."

"What?" asked Benny.

"I wanna look at the house."

Calvin lit up a smoke. "That sounds dangerous."

Dressed in tan scrubs and neon green Chucks, Grace took off from the porch and made her way across the street.

"Shit," said Benny, fumbling to get after her.

Calvin followed too, wondering how he had become entangled in another one of Grace's misadventures. For someone so intelligent, she had some really stupid ideas. Not so much stupid, but reckless. They'd almost had to fight a biker gang once because of her mouth.

Through the side, Grace climbed into the property, heedless of the shifting debris. She made it into what remained of the house and pulled out her phone, turning on the flashlight feature. Only the back half of the house was gone. Both Calvin and Benny followed, far more tentative.

The place appeared to be stripped, no doors, cabinets, pipes, or anything. It made sense, since all that could be repurposed or sold off. Benny yelled at Grace as she went for the stairs, but she only went up far enough to glance around. There was nothing here of any interest.

Then she spied a doorway leading to the basement.

"This is super dumb, babe," said Benny.

"I know," she replied, heading down.

Benny shook his head. "Fuck that, I'm not going."

Calvin sighed. He hated getting in the middle of their disputes. Still, he didn't want to feel responsible if his friend got hurt. Swearing, he followed her down.

In the basement, it was cleared out, like the rest of the house. Nothing interesting. It was your basic dirty cement floor with brick walls and exposed pipes above. He was about to call for Grace, when he found her at a far wall. She just stood there, shinning her light. Dirt and dust swirled around the beam, and the entire structure creaked above. A car driving past sent a flicker of illumination through the small cracked window.

"We've got to go, Grace," he said.

"Look at this."

Calvin came up beside her. What he thought was the far wall had crumbled apart, probably due to the seismic force of the demolition directly above. It revealed a small room beyond, not much bigger than what might have been considered a walk-in closet. Entirely of windowless stone, it held only one thing.

What looked to be a sarcophagus.

"What the literal fuck," said Calvin.

"Is… is that a coffin?"

"No, it's a sarcophagus. Coffins are buried."

"This isn't buried?"

"You know what I mean. Regardless, I didn't sign up for any vampires, so let's get out of here."

"Wait," she said, moving closer.

Grace began to examine it, bringing her phone flashlight closer. The thing was huge, easily eight feet long, three feet wide, and rising four feet off the ground. The rough shape of a head and shoulders tapered to slightly narrower feet. Composed of a dark gray stone, there looked like there might have been some type of raised lettering along the edge at one point. Whatever it had said, it was now unreadable. A very definite seam was apparent though, a means to open it.

Grace pushed on the top.

"What are you doing?" I said, grabbing her arm.

"Trying to open it."

"Are you insane? Have you never seen a horror movie? That's how we get monsters, Grace! For once, don't be you."

She frowned at him, and stepped back. "I'm telling the construction crew about this."

"Fine. Let's go."

TRUE TO HER WORD, Grace took the next day off from work. She was up bright and early as any other day, but instead of heading out, she blew up Calvin's phone until he answered.

"Dear Christ, what do you want?"

"Come outside! I have coffee and donuts."

Calvin threw on clothes and stumbled downstairs. He found his neighbor waiting for him on his porch with the promised treats and a huge grin.

"How do you function at this ungodly hour?" he asked.

"It's seven a.m., Calvin," she said. "A lot of people are up by now."

"Madness."

They munched on donut holes and guzzled dark roast until the crew showed up about thirty minutes later. Before Calvin could say anything, Grace launched herself off the porch towards the trucks. He followed her with a sigh and came to find her in an animated conversation with the foreman he had spoken to previously.

He was less than pleased to discovered they had entered the property, but even more distraught when Calvin confirmed Grace's wild claims there was a sarcophagus in the basement. The demolition was on a strict deadline and something like this could throw the whole project off.

The foreman began to climb into the house, followed by two of his men. Grace fell in behind, and there was some argument about her coming along. As much as Calvin liked to give his neighbor grief about being a spaz, she had risen to be one of the youngest medical administrators in the state. Her professional side kicked in, and she dressed down the entire crew, explaining the significance of the find. Somehow in the span of two minutes, not only was she leading the expedition to the basement, now wearing a helmet, but Calvin was allowed to trudge along as well.

The house still seemed as sturdy as it had last night, but in the light, one could see just how precarious their situation was inside the structure. The ceiling was ready to cave in at any moment, and the south wall was visibly crumbling. That south wall was right above the entrance to the hidden room in the basement.

Flashlights on, descending into the basement proper, the

foreman was aghast seeing the sarcophagus with his own eyes. With a great deal of hand-wringing, he made it blatantly clear that he would happily bury the thing and forget about it if he could. Neither of his crewmen seemed to care either way.

"This project has to move forward, on schedule," said the foreman. "If I happened to drop a hundred dollar bill in the direction of each of you, what are the chances we could all forget about this?"

Calvin shook his head. Everyone in this town was corrupt, but he couldn't blame the guy. Nobody comes to work and expects this.

"Sure," said Grace. "But you gotta open it first."

"Grace, what did I tell you about horror movies?"

"I'll always wonder and it'll drive me insane."

The foreman held up his hands. "That can be done. You two go get some crowbars."

Money was accidentally dropped and picked up while the crewman retrieved the tools. They returned with a sack's worth of implements, and set on it. The others tried to light their job with the flashlights as best they could.

At first, the endeavor didn't look like it was going to be successful. The crowbars weren't working deep enough into the narrow seam, and only scraping the stone. Finally, one of the crewmen tried a different angle as the other slammed the back of it with a hammer. That got it in. Once wedged under the lip and lifted slightly, another lever was applied.

The second the lid was shifted a few inches off to the side, the basement was overcome by the smell. It was the stench of spoiled meat and disease, but also as if it had been covered in spices. Clove and ginger, something undeterminable. Maybe citrus? Calvin couldn't help but think of holiday cookies.

A few more grunts, and the lid was pushed off. Everyone tentatively leaned in, flashlights aglow.

It was empty. Just some black sludge at the bottom.

"Well, that was anticlimactic," said one of the crewmen.

"If that concludes our business, I'd like to..." began the foreman.

"Wait!" said Grace. "I'll be right back!"

She shot out of the room. Everyone gawked as she disappeared up the stairs.

"Is she always like that?" asked the foreman.

"Yep."

The remaining four stayed away from the sarcophagus, although Calvin did snap some pictures on his phone. He promised the foreman he wouldn't say anything, just wanted them for his own reasons. Honestly, he knew Grace would regret not getting them later.

He ran his finger along the carved letter found on the outside, and found the same on the inside. It was somewhat more legible within, but still not in any language he was familiar with. It looked to be almost runic, but he far from any expert.

A bang from upstairs, and Grace came clomping back down the steps. Now she held a mason jar with its lid, beaming proudly.

Calvin frowned. "What are you going to do with that?"

"Getting a sample."

"Gross."

Grace leaned over the side and scooped up the sludge from the bottom into the jar. She managed to get it three quarters full before she decided that was enough. In her zeal, she also managed to get it all over her hands.

"Uh, you need to go wash your hands with fire," said Calvin.

Grace examined her hands and made a face. "Yeah, I may have gone too far."

"You, too far? No!"

The foreman rubbed his face. "Are we done here?"

CALVIN WAS ALREADY SITTING on Benny's porch when he got home from work later that afternoon. As soon as he climbed out of his car and saw the look on his friend's face, he knew something was up.

"What?"

"So, it was an eventful morning."

With a groan he came up the steps and took the mug of coffee offered. Taking a sip, Benny pulled out a pack of cigarettes. Lighting one up, he gestured for Calvin to continue.

Calvin filled him in on what had happened with the construction crew and the sarcophagus. He took it all relatively well, up until the point Grace was digging around in the sludge with a jar. At this point Benny was rubbing his temples and swearing under his breath.

"Where is she now," he asked.

"I assume she's still napping. She started to feel like shit about two hours ago."

"Of course! Who the hell knows what that stuff was, and she had it all over her. She is the dumbest smart person I've ever met."

"I mean, I agree one hundred percent. I just thought you should have a head's up."

"Thanks, man."

They had another smoke, then Calvin headed back over to his house. He had kind of wanted to hang out more, but he knew it wasn't Benny's job to entertain him. Back in his own place, he looked around and tried to decide what to do.

He was currently all caught up on his freelance work. There was always portfolio work he could do, but his heart simply was in it that night. He had a few books on his iPad, but nothing that looked all that interesting. If he tried to watch something, he only spent an hour scrolling through streaming sites trying to find something. Social media only depressed him anymore.

Mostly because of Lucy.

They had been together for four years, and split almost nine months ago. She had gotten a job offer across the state, and the moment it came down the line, things had devolved. Everything had been an argument, everything a stressor. None of it should have been that big a deal. Calvin would've quit his job or just relocated, already working at home at that point, then sold the house. He would've moved for her. But she didn't know if she wanted the job, and didn't seem to understand that indecision was problematic for him. He had to make arrangements. She rented month to month, always wanting to keep her independence.

Well, she ended up getting it.

Looking back, he knew things had been bad for a while, but it all still stung. And now he didn't know what to do with himself half the time. He could only watch so many reruns on streaming.

It was warm for early September, so he left the door open. A nice breeze came through the screen as he sat down with his iPad and started mashing apps, looking to waste time until he got a better idea. Zeus wandered up and screeched at him for no reason before going to peer out at the window.

Calvin was about to light up a cigarette when he caught a whiff of the sludge. Rotten meat and holiday cookies. It was faint, but unmistakable. Then it was gone. Going to the door, he gave a sniff, but there was nothing. He wondered if it was just some kind of memory before slumping back onto the couch.

Knowing he would regret it, he pulled up one of the dating apps he had already deleted twice.

ANOTHER DAY OF NOISE. Calvin walked back inside his house, grumbling to himself. He had just spoken to the foreman who had broken the bad news. Two of his men had called in sick, cutting his team in half. While they would get the house torn down today, there was no way they could get the debris hauled away until Monday. Calvin hadn't said anything about Grace falling ill, but wondered if it was the same two guys who had been down in the basement. Odd that he and the foreman appeared fine.

That portfolio needed to be tackled, but Calvin really wasn't in the headspace for it. He shuffled back into the kitchen and retrieved his second cup of coffee as Zeus scowled at him from the stairs. Most of the work in it leaned towards the darker side. He had wanted to start getting gigs doing book covers and album art, but nothing of the sort had really materialized. It was all the same type of clients from before, corporate stooges who were convinced a rebranding of their company would jump quarterly profits. Change the font slightly, make the blue a brighter hue, tilt the image fifteen degrees. Applause all around for the breath-taking new diaper logo!

Calvin had long ago realized he had no need for a dinning room, and converted it into a workspace. The spare bedroom he could have used for an office upstairs simply hadn't been big enough, so a spare bedroom it stayed. Lucy had tried to tell him it was unhealthy to have his work life so meshed with his home life, but he had never listened. It wasn't until he had begun doing the bulk of his job from home that he under-stood. Sitting at the computer, he spent twenty minutes scrolling through different Spotify playlists and glancing through the living room out the window.

This state of procrastination is why he noticed a car pull into the driveway across at Benny and Grace's place. Looking for any distraction, he got up and went to the door. Sure, he was being nosy, but he didn't think they would mind.

Honestly, Calvin didn't care. Anything to keep him away from work.

It was their friend Mia. Calvin had been friends with her way back in the day, but had recently become reacquainted when she had started working with Grace. The stylish blonde stood by her car and surveyed the demolition with a distain that was clear from across the street.

Calvin hadn't even noticed Grace's car in the driveway when he had been talking to the foreman earlier. Their garage was so full of junk, they couldn't park either vehicle in there anymore. But it wasn't even noon yet, and she should've been at work. He wondered if he should see if Grace was still sick.

Calvin hesitated at the door. Mia was some kind of therapist, working for the state. He wasn't entirely sure what she did, but it sounded pretty heavy. Her reasoning for being there could be personal, or work-related. Or both. He let go of the handle and went back to the computer. It was honestly none of his business and he'd ask Benny if his wife was doing better later.

Stupid portfolio.

SOME DESIGNS GOT DONE and a turkey sandwich was eaten. Hours passed and Calvin forgot about Mia. The crew left next door for the day and the couch called to him. Lying down, he threw on a Carpenter Brut playlist before he closed his eyes.

The dreams came almost immediately.

The forest was ancient, primeval. Massive pine trees soared high, their branches covered in snow. The ground was frozen hard, snowdrifts deep where the wind had found purchase. The underbrush looked brittle, the bark almost a shade a blue.

The scene changed, moved. The landscape was still rugged wilderness, still frigid, but now had additional colors. Red splatters painted the ground, the warm blood melting the snow into the dirt and mixing into mud. The blood dripped from the evergreen needles, pooled in footprints gouged into the earth. There was more. Flesh and skin, bones and offal. Broken and torn pieces of people lay steaming in the cold air.

People who continued to live. They squirmed and moaned as their bodies began to fuse, the meat of one stitching together with that of another. Bones reshaped into something new, muscles crawling like worms. A man rose to his feet, no longer a man, his face full of tongues. Something like laughter erupted from his head, eliciting the same joy from his kin. A girl child wobbled out from the trees, her lower half an abomination.

Pulled back, there was a destination. No, a home. A stone monolith that stood in the forest, surrounded by torches and blood. Although much larger than the sarcophagus, it was undeniably the same dark gray stone.

Calvin awoke with a start, bashing his elbow on the coffee table. Yelping at the pain, he grabbed at his cup to make sure he didn't spill it. Most of the dream was fading, he only recalled it had been creepy.

He was definitely listening to Lana Del Rey next time.

***

WHATEVER ACTION MOVIE he had thrown on was absolutely terrible. The dialogue seemed to have been penned by teenagers, and the plot cobbled together by people with only a vague understanding of how the world worked. Escapist entertainment was great, but there was a point when it became ridiculous. Currently the hero had a bomb in his heart that could only be removed with a laser conveniently designed by the love interest's dead father, who was also a secret Nazi. Jesus Christ.

Halfway through, Calvin turned it off. He wasn't even sure what was happening. It was the third movie he had watched that night since waking up from his nap, only taking a break to scrounge up a snack. It should've been a more productive night, but then again he could say that about most of his nights.

Gathering up his chip bag, salsa bowl, and drink, he was about to head into the kitchen when he heard a noise outside: the shifting of debris next door. He set all the stuff back down on the coffee table and went to the door. There wasn't much to see; it was near midnight and the streets dark. He opened the door and peered around at the demolished house.

Grace stood on the wreckage and appeared to be gesturing to Mia to move a few bricks. Mia – and her husband, Kurt – moved a few out of the way, and begun digging deeper. It was too dark to see well, but they all looked filthy. A big plastic scrub bucket perched on the rubble next to Grace.

Calvin stepped out onto the porch, about to ask them what they were doing, when Benny materialized from the gloom across the street. He looked like Grace felt earlier. Pale and almost rubbery, he slinked closer.

"Hey, didn't realize you were still up."

Calvin pointed at the house. "What the fuck are you guys doing?"

"Annette wanted some bricks for her garden."

Annette, Mia's little sister. Super hot, and slightly crazy. Knowing her, that sounded legit.

"Okay, why are you doing it now instead of during the day when you can see?"

Benny gave a weird little shrug. "You know Grace."

He did. Something about his neighbor was off, though. The way she was standing there overseeing the other two working put a bad taste in his mouth. She turned to look at him, her gaze cold. Then she broke into that normal grin or hers and waved. It all felt very calculated somehow, faked.

She bounded off the rubble, followed by Mia and Kurt. They all began to head back over to the house, bucket in hand. Calvin worried she had been digging for more of that sludge, but there was no way she could have gotten deep enough. As the others reached the porch, Benny turned around in the middle of the street.

"Did you want to come over?"

"Eh, no thanks. Watching a movie."

"We'll see you tomorrow with everyone else."

"Everyone else?"

But it was too late, he was already heading inside. Calvin stood on his porch, wondering what the hell he had just witnessed.

THE COW WOBBLED, *barely able to hold up its rumbling body. Eyes wide, the corners of its mouth had torn from screaming out sounds no bovine creature had ever emitted. Legs shattered as it fell, the belly rupturing open. Instead of intestine spilling out, it was something else.*

Pink, whipping tentacles lifted the creature back up off the ground, useless legs now dangling. Some began to strip what was once a cow of its skin with barbed tips, while other grew large eyes on their ends. That high-pitched sound still wailed from its mouth as the jaw pulled back even farther.

Most of the remaining herd had fled towards the mountains. Ambling high in the tree line, gifted with dozens of eyes, it followed. It needed more, it needed better.

Calvin woke in time to make it to the garbage can in his bed room. Fortunately he had just emptied it last week.

An hour later, he was sitting on his couch with a cup of coffee and scrolling through social media. The nightmare had faded, but not the sensation. He knew he'd had two in a row now, something about snow and bloody flesh in the first. It was easy enough to chalk it all up to stress and that damn sarcophagus, but they were still disconcerting.

Calvin didn't like to think he was stalking his ex, per se,

but he was definitely creeping. Two weeks ago she had posted a photo of her out at a bar with a group of friends, a very attractive man leaning in behind her and hand on her shoulder. He shouldn't have been jealous, but he had drank himself into a haze that night. Swearing off her accounts for a week, he'd been back to checking them since. Calvin knew it wasn't healthy, but he didn't get out much, and didn't know how to move on.

He was still stewing over that photo when there was a bang on his door.

Calvin squinted at the clock. Noon? Who the hell would knock on his door this early? Benny and Grace knew better. Chances were it was somebody trying to sell him religion. Annoyed, he climbed off the couch, ready to yell at someone.

He opened the door to find a husky black man standing there with a duffle bag in one hand and case of beer at his feet.

"Motherfucker, were you still asleep?"

Calvin ran his hand through his hair. "Anton, why are you on my porch?"

"Because those assholes across the street aren't answering the door."

Calvin shook his head, confused. He let Anton in, and grabbed the beer. His oldest friend tossed the duffle on the loveseat, plopping down beside it. Calvin sat the beer over by the television and took his seat back on the couch.

"Okay, let's try this again," said Calvin. "I'm obviously missing something."

"Benny texted me last night, said they're having some big shindig today. Says come in early. Shit, the drive in is nearly three hours, so I leave at nine. Get here, they don't answer even though their cars are out front. So, here we are."

"He did say something cryptic about, I dunno, people last night."

"That's helpful, thanks."

"Go fuck yourself. Coffee?"

The two strolled into the kitchen to find a clean mug. They talked about work; Anton was a computer analyst. He was happily divorced and purposely didn't bring up Lucy, knowing it was still a sore topic for Calvin. Instead, they talked about movies, diving into all the titles they had digested in the past weeks. It had always been a shared passion of the two, everything from horror and science fiction, to noir and action. Calvin made sure to tell him about the train wreck he'd try to watch the previous evening.

"Aw hell, yeah! I tried that one, too. Did you see who the director was? He's done decent shit. I assume coke was involved this time."

Calvin laughed. "That, or a massive paycheck."

"People do some dumb shit."

"Speaking of, I haven't told you about the sarcophagus."

"The what?"

Calvin filled him in, starting at the beginning with the demolition crew waking him up, Grace's discovery, and ending with everyone playing in the debris last night. Anton stared at him the entire time, silent. When he finished, Calvin sat back and lit up a cigarette.

Anton nodded and pulled out his vape. "Right. Have you learned nothing? I know it's your white person instinct to run face first towards creepy shit, but you've been around me since we were seven. Remember when Megan Vance wanted to go hang out in the graveyard?"

"One, Megan Vance got arrested by the cops, not molested by ghosts like you said would happen. Two, I wanted nothing to do with this fuckery. I got dragged into it by Grace the Unicorn Princess having another one of her adventures."

"All irrelevant, dickface," said Anton. "Two situations, both two major problems. You don't realize how sketch a situation is, and you want to be a hero."

Calvin lowered his head. "I don't want to be a hero."

"Brother, that's the only reason you stayed with Lucy for so long. You wanted to take care of her."

Calvin changed to topic, and Anton rolled with it. He could tell he may have pushed his friend too far. They had been through a lot over the years – shared grief, laughter, fights, weddings, all of it. Anton let him pull up a Spotify playlist and show him some songs, content not to say another word about it.

A COUPLE HOURS had dropped off when they heard a car door slam out front. Anton twisted around on the loveseat and glanced out the front window. He started laughing and grabbed for his vape.

"What?" asked Calvin.

He followed Anton outside and saw Cam and Levi heading down the sidewalk towards the house across the street. Cam had gone to school with all of them; Levi her husband for some years. They were a hysterical couple, both in personality and appearance. Cam was tiny and curvy while Levi towered at almost six and a half feet.

"Hey you little shit, you still have to climb that mountain for sex?" Anton yelled.

Cam burst into giggles. "Get over here you asshole!"

She hugged him as Calvin walked up and shook Levi's hand. "How are those Viking raids going?"

Levi sighed. "Pillaging just isn't what it used to be."

Calvin laughed. "I hear Viagra might help with that."

Cam smacked him. "Calvin!"

"Not to interrupt this awkward banter we have here," said Anton. "But I'm guessing Benny texted you?"

"Yeah, why?" asked Cam.

"I showed up a while back and no one answered the door."

"That's weird. Maybe they weren't home."

"Cars are here."

Cam scrunched up her face. "I hope they're okay. We better go knock."

Before they could even reach the porch, Mia came out. Calvin stood there stunned. Mia had always been an attractive woman, but he had always viewed her more like a sister. Their relationship tended to be tempestuous, constantly bickering as far back as high school. However, the Mia on the porch now was remarkably different than the one he had known for years, omehow absolutely gorgeous and utterly disgusting at the same time. She swayed slightly as Cam and Levi walked up to the front of the house. Her skin was flawless but it had a slight sheen to it, almost a gloss. It was the same with her hair, almost as if it had gel in it, yet retained its volume. Her eyes seemed bigger, mouth a little wider, all of her proportions were somehow exaggerated in a way Calvin couldn't quite put his finger on. It was alluring and unnerving.

Cam was talking to Mia, but Calvin wasn't really paying attention to what was being said. He caught something about a "new skin lotion," but clearly Cam wasn't buying it. The skinny jean and skin-tight tank top wasn't leaving much to the imagination, clothing that Mia wasn't one to usually wear. While he had conflicted feelings, Anton had no such qualms.

"Man, Mia's banging today."

Calvin didn't reply. Instead he watched as she ushered Cam and Levi inside. Anton started to follow, but she held out a hand. Her fingers looked far longer and more slender than they should.

"Benny and Grace have this whole theme thing going on," said Mia. "We're bringing people in early, but in shifts. You'll see! We'll have you over later and it'll be awesome. Promise."

She winked at him and lead the other two inside, closing the door behind her.

Anton stood on the sidewalk, hands in the air. "What the literal fuck!"

"This is super shady."

"No Calvin, it's just rude," Anton replied, storming back across the street.

Following him, he stopped to examine his own hands. Calvin tried to believe it was all in his head, just paranoia. His fingers weren't longer, thinner. They weren't bending in strange, unnatural ways. No, everything was fine.

Inside, Anton had cracked a beer and proceeded to start drinking.

"I'm going to need one or eight of those," said Calvin.

MANY BEERS LATER, Anton was still pissed. He had always been easily offended, and quick to hold a grudge far longer than was necessary. At some point, he had ordered pizza, bitching about the situation between slices.

Calvin hadn't eaten much. He had stopped staring at his fingers but still felt off: dizziness along with bouts of nausea. Body aches with a throbbing in his head. On any other day, he would have thought he was coming down with the flu. This was different.

Anton kept downing beers and getting riled up. Calvin wasn't entirely sure what had so insulted his friend, and he didn't really care. It was hard enough to stay coherent. He simply didn't have the energy to soothe Anton's delicate sensibilities as he grew more intoxicated.

"Calling me all the way down here and then making me wait while they play fiddledicks? What the fuck is all that about?"

Calvin's head lolled back on the couch. "I dunno, man."

"I had a date this weekend, ya know. I rescheduled that

shit for you guys. And that's all good, but I just want a little consideration. A little communication."

"It's crazy."

At some point Anton either realized Calvin was passing out or had worked himself up enough to take his grievances across the street. Hours had passed when Calvin awoke to the sound of someone knocking on his door. It was almost ten, and most of the beer was gone along with his friend.

Stumbling to the door, Calvin's head pounded. Ready to banish whoever he found there, that idea evaporated when he saw it was Annette. She was a few years younger than Mia and looked similar, though much shorter, with dark hair and dark eyes. They loose crop top she had on barely concealed anything, nor did it hide the same sheen to her skin that her sister had shone.

"You look like shit," she said, brushing black curls out of her face.

"Uh, I think I'm getting the flu."

"That sucks. Can I come in?"

Calvin nodded, opening the door. She slinked past him and glanced around. A little smile played at the corner of her lips, and he felt something tugging inside himself.

"Anton was here earlier," he said. "Not sure where he went."

"Oh, he's over at Benny's. Came over and threw a little tantrum."

"Sounds about right."

She walked around, inspecting some of his artwork. Annette had never been here before. She had been too young for them to know each other back in school, everyone in their early thirties and her in only her mid-twenties. Mia had introduced her to everyone back during quarantine, via Zoom chats, and they'd only hung out once since then.

She had those same indefinable qualities that Mia had displayed before. Glistening skin, exaggerated proportions, fluid movements, yes those were all there. But it was more than that. Pieces of a much larger puzzle.

Calvin found his head in his hands. Was his head mushy, or was there something wrong with his hands? He staggered and fell into Annette.

"Let's get you upstairs."

He wasn't even sure how he got up the steps. She kept whispering things to him, salacious and enticing words of encouragement. Pushed against the hallway wall, she began kissing him. Her lips tasted of spoiled meat and holiday cookies. It was foul, but he kissed her deeper.

In the bedroom, Annette pulled his clothes off as she stripped off her own. Her body was gorgeous, almost unnaturally so. Calvin fell back and she climbed on top of him, kissing, touching. It wasn't until he ran his hands across her that he realized he could feel the slick, gel-like sweat on her body. Instead of disgusting him, it made him harder. She reached down and slid him inside, holding down his shoulders as she rode him.

Calvin's mind swum with ecstasy and madness. His hands reached up for her breasts, but swore his fingers were bending and reshaping. His eyes drifted up to Annette's face, but then were thrown back in the moment. The scent grew stronger, more cloying.

Annette began to moan. "Ah Kullith, as we give ours, give unto us. Oh god, all the kisses!"

The pain in his skull returned. His bones were on fire. Yet the pleasure raced through him, something more than he had ever experienced from sex before. More words spilled from Annette, but Calvin didn't understand any of them. He didn't understand anything. His body was in a state of chaos.

Then his orgasm came and he passed out once again.

THE FROZEN LAND. The ground hard-packed and covered with a deep snow where unencumbered by the dense trees. Ahead there is a lake, a bowl of ice. Even at its depth it is solid. The surface is wind-blown, one of the few open areas in this frigid wastelands.

A lone figure stalks across it, massive by the standards of any era. Without clothing, its form is clear and horrifying. An amalgamation of many, it is comprised of at least five humans, perhaps more. Their bodies have fused together to create a singular entity, bones and flesh melded into something new. It lumbers along with purpose, unaffected by the cold.

With six eyes it turns to peer at the heavens. At Calvin. "Kullith."

Another nightmare. Calvin laid there and stared at his bedroom ceiling. Gritting his teeth, he raised his hands to inspect his fingers. They were fine.

He crawled out of bed and got dressed. That general sense of feeling like he'd fallen down a flight of steps wasn't as bad as before, but his head still ached. At some point Annette had left, but that wasn't really a concern at this point. All that mattered was getting as much caffeine and nicotine into his system as soon as possible.

This living room was a mess. Ignoring it, he swiped his smokes off the coffee table and headed into the kitchen. Robotically, he began to prepare the coffee began to be prepared. The house was quiet, Anton either asleep or still across the street. Calvin pulled some sweeten creamer out of the fridge and puffed on a cigarette until he'd filled his mug.

Back on the couch, the whole living room stank of stale beer. A glance at his phone told him it was past noon. Although he felt better than he had last night, it seemed likely that he had come down with something. What worried him was that it had been contracted from that damn sarcophagus. A quick glance in the phone's camera revealed he didn't appear to have the same sheen or features that Mia and

Annette did. Was that all even related? What about the fingers?

Calvin snuffed out his cigarette, exhausted. Lying back, mind whirling, he fell asleep again as his skin shifted.

———

THE FLESH ROLLED like ocean waves, peeling open to reveal a wide mouth line with not teeth, but fingers. The woman fell to her knees, and smiled, tears rolling down her face. She did not tremble from the cold, but in anticipation. The moon was blotted out from the sky as the meat of many lunged forward.

Calvin was growing numb to the nightmares. He wasn't so dense that he couldn't see there was a story there, but he'd be damned if he knew what it was. Between them and all the growing weirdness, it was growing harder to deny everything was linked to the nonsense found next door.

Speaking of growing weirdness, all the cars were still parked on the street. Everybody was still over at Benny's place. In fact, it looked there were more cars dotting the neighborhood now then there had been last night. He hadn't had any contact with anyone since Annette, and couldn't imagine what was going on at this point.

Maybe it was time to find out.

Calvin grabbed his smokes and phone, and headed over. There wasn't anyone out on the street, but that wasn't terribly unusual for six pm on a Sunday. Still, he climbed slowly up onto their porch, looking around. The door was open.

"Uh, hello?" he called out.

He opened the door and stepped in, almost immediately tripping over a pair of legs. Jumping back, he found a young woman laying there, half naked. She had on shoes and a shirt, but that was it. He didn't recognize her, but she gazed up at him and smiled before her eyelids fluttered. She was out.

Turning, he found Cam passed out on Levi, both

completely naked on a couch. There were a few more people strewn around the room in various states of undress, most in a daze. One was smoking a joint, another playing on her phone. Calvin kept going down the hall and passed the dining room, only to find more people. Again, most were unconscious, but two were engaged in the most lazy sex act he'd ever witnessed. He wasn't sure what they were on, but was surprised they could move.

Calvin stood there dumbfounded. Had all this just been some drug-fueled orgy? Maybe he had just been tripping this whole time.

Making his way into the kitchen, he expected to find more of the same: stoned people licking whipped cream off one another or something. Instead he found Grace standing there completely naked eating a piece of raw meat.

Nothing about it was sexy.

Her tall, slender body had gone through many changes. Instead of simply having that moist coating and odd dimensions, she barely looked human. Grace no longer had any trace of body hair, what was on her head appearing like a singular mass. All of her resembled something gelatinous, like a human shaped out of spam. The white of her large eyes were full of her blood, the same blood that spilled from her mouth with every bite she took of the raw chicken.

Calvin tried to process what he was seeing. He tried to overlap what he was currently experiencing as Grace with all the memories of past Grace. These two things were not meshing well. They both stood there gawking at each other, as she continued to eat.

"Um, you should probably cook that," was all he could come up with.

Grace laughed. "I've always liked you, Calvin. You've been a good neighbor. I'm glad you were with me when the new world began."

"What the fuck are you talking about? What the hell is going on?"

Grace frowned. "You've been touched. I know you've heard the word."

"You mean Annette? Yeah, I mean that was awesome, but I would've enjoyed it more if I wasn't freaking out. Did you guys fucking dose me with something? I'm down to party, but ya know, consent is cool and all."

Grace backed away muttering to herself. "I don't understand. My flesh can feel his."

"Seriously Grace, something's wrong with you. You look… not good. You do realize you're naked, right? Where's Benny?"

Grace smiled. Her teeth were perfectly smooth behind all the blood. Too perfect. "Benny's with me, with us. As you should be."

"What's that supposed to mean?"

"I know you've had a glimpse. The Flesh, The Legion, The Hive. Kullith. Something greater than humanity, beyond the confines of this planet. It creates as it destroys, blooms as it breaks. It evolves feeble meat and makes it strong, takes the limited strings of consciousness and weaves them into a tapestry. We are united."

Calvin backed away. "That's madness."

"Free will, individuality, scurrying around scared and anxious? That's madness. But soon we'll all be a piece to a greater whole. We should have been a long time ago, but it was cold when Kullith came and ignorant men thought they had defeated fate."

The nightmares.

Calvin started moving out of the kitchen.

"You know I'm telling you the truth, I can see it on your face," said Grace. "Here, let me show you how true it is on *my* face."

Grace began to blossom into something new, some new

form. It was one that was wet and rancid. She grew taller, more lengthened, her limbs developing additional joints while somehow being more fluid. Hips wider, waist narrower, her nipples became larger and more pointed as her skin grew a dark pink with a mottled gray like that of steak left out. Every part of her was covered in a sticky, viscous substance. Finally, her head opened up like a flower, meat petals lined with rows of teeth clustered with a circle of those large, now unblinking eyes in the middle. In the very center, her tongue rolled out and licked at one of the eyes.

Calvin ran.

He made it halfway down the hall before Benny smashed into him from the side, out of the dining room. Calvin pushed him back and tried to regain his balance. His neighbor looked worse than Mia had the day before. Calvin raced around the Dinning room table past the fireplace and grabbed one of the pokers.

"Benny, don't do this!"

Benny didn't say anything. He couldn't. His teeth were dripping out of his mouth. He lunged around the table and Calvin brought the poker down hard on his friend's head. Instead of the resistance you'd expect from a skull, there was a soft squish.

Benny leapt back. The poker hung, imbedded in Benny's skull by a good four inches, deep within the soft meat. His head had taken it like pressing a finger into a cake. His face had deformed along with the intrusion, his eye now leaking out as if it was jelly down his face. None of it seemed to hurt him, Benny only fingering the poker as if he was confused.

Calvin screamed and ran for the door. Blocked by the massive Levi, still naked, he bolted upstairs. There were more people upstairs. He didn't think Benny and Grace had this many friends, wondered where they all had come from.

What looked like a teenage girl smashed him in the shoulder with a lamp, and he staggered through a half-closed door. Struggling to pull a shard of glass out, he spun to find Annette laying on a bed with Mia attending to her.

"Oh Calvin, you gifted me with your seed!" squealed Annette. "I had no idea I would be so blessed."

Annette was very, very pregnant. Her belly was huge, swollen beyond any normal size, let alone what it should have been from a day ago. The skin was stretch paper thin with small tears throughout, a gritty yellow pus leaking from her in myriad places. That now familiar scent was strong in the room as Mia played midwife, Annette beginning to wail as her bulbous form shook.

Calvin backed up against the wall. Horrified, he watched as her screams rose, as she split open. From between her legs and up her center, she tore all the way to her breasts and split open. Liquified intestines and congealed blood, bones that had rearranged and turned to chalk, all of it had become nutrient for the clutch of quivering eggs that emerged within the red slurry.

They began to come alive, easily two dozen tiny black monstrosities writhing with thin tendrils and covered with blinking, polyp-like eyes. A few skittered up Annette, who was still somehow alive, and laughing like a lunatic.

"My babies! My beautiful little miracles!"

Something in Calvin fully cracked as he witnessed this. Seeing Annette splayed apart, cooing over abomination he had helped to spawn, was simply too much. Benny broke into the room and he jammed a shard of glass into his friend's throat. Anton pushed in close behind. Anton, now glistening. Calvin pushed an air conditioner out of the window and jumped. He should have injured himself, broken a leg. Instead his legs simply bent.

He wobbled back across the street, laughing, crying, feeling no pain.

THE HUMAN STEPPED AWAY from his companions, nervous but determined to show bravery. The rock sat in a deep crater, and the warrior gawked up at the sky as he made his way down. Large and dark grey, it sat still steaming in the cold morning. Reaching the bottom, one could feel the warmth radiating from it. The warrior drew closer, reaching out. As soon as he touched it, the change was immediate.

Calvin sat up and looked for his cigarettes. He thought he may have finally began to piece together a story. A meteorite hit earth a long time ago, who knows when. When a human touched it, they became infected. At some point, the meteorite became the monolith, and worshipped. Later, the monolith was hollowed out and turned into the sarcophagus. Had they figured out how to trap it? He didn't see how that could be possible. Everything about this story he had cobbled together seemed full of holes.

After he got home last night, he had used what little strength he had left to barricade his house. It might not make a difference, but it made him feel better. Then he called the cops. Drugs seemed like a good enough story. He threw guns in, too. Sure enough, two cops cars materialized within minutes. They never left.

Dead or pulled to the dark side, Calvin didn't care. He was on his own. Now that he was up again, he started packing a bag, ready to bail out. All he had to do was make it to his car. It was parked outside of his house, just jump in and go. Anywhere, any destination better than here.

Looking for his spare charging cord, he got a text alert. It was Mia.

He sank into the couch as he read.

They had sabotaged his car, and threatened to cut his internet if he tried to go anywhere. Anton would know exactly how to do that. Mia said they would leave him alone if he simply stayed put and left them be. Oh, and they had greeted the demolition crew when they returned this morning.

Calvin texted back, asking why he was feeling some of the effects but not a pod person like them. To his surprise, she gave him an answer. She replied it was different for different people. It took longer for some, and never for others. In the end, he had seen Kullith reborn on earth and he would be unified.

That was enough for Mia. For what was once Grace.

Yes, his body was changing, bending and beginning to get the sheen, but he felt no allegiance to some alien disease locked in the basement next door. There was nothing like that. Kullith could get fucked.

He began to search the internet for any way he could find to stop this, clues to where this may have popped up before. Although he made a cup of coffee, he didn't touch it, nor did he light up a single cigarette. Calvin didn't even notice those urges had vanished.

A FEW MORE HOURS HAD PASSED, AND things had grown chaotic outside. Those across the street were no longer hiding. There were at least a hundred of them gathered throughout the street, many of them far from human now. Calvin wrapped his worm-like fingers around the curtain and peered out.

Benny had become something entirely without bones or true form, bouncing and rolling place to place, while Anton was merely a mass of warts and lesions. Levi hadn't changed much, still strolling around naked, but Cam seemed quite elated with the tentacles she had sprouted in place of her hands. Many had massive growths of flesh that throbbed and spurted blood, while others appeared boneless like Benny. Others glistened hairless and slick as Mia and Annette had.

Mia came out from around the side of the house, chanting the name of their alien god. She dripped with that thick residue, her skin now almost transparent. Behind her came Grace, now larger and even more inhuman. She milked her own breasts, baptizing the faithful into mutated forms with just a mouthful.

In the shadows, spider-like creatures the size of large dogs cavorted and chittered with each over. All Calvin could do was sigh upon realizing they were his children.

None of it horrified him anymore. Not even when they began to drag out humans from surrounding areas and force them on their knees before Grace for the sacrament. He watched people struggle, begging and fighting, as they took her milk. Each one came away devoted.

Some of these people had families. Benny had a brother. Mia a son. Cam and Levi two children of their own. And yet an infant was laid into Grace's arm and feed, it's small body forever transformed. They were all children of Kullith now.

Calvin sat there, feeling nothing. Then Annette walked out the front door. Somehow she was alive, healed. Her body had stitched itself back together and glistened, although not nearly to the degree of her sister's. Instead, a red scar ran from between her legs up to between her breasts where she had split open. She smiled, radiant in both her belief and beauty. Holding up a hand, one of their children crawled under the porch roof and nuzzled against her fingers.

Calvin watched this, crushed by an onslaught of mixed emotions, feeling for the first time in hours. All the other atrocities in the neighborhood disappeared, the monsters meaningless. There was just Annette and his child.

He let the curtain drop and went for the door.

Kullith could have the world, he wanted this.

2

I SEE YOU BETWEEN THE STARS

I SUPPOSE it started at breakfast.

My tray of food looked like everyone else's that morning, whatever the station's chef had decided to prep for us. Some kind of wrap filled with leafy greens and a mystery protein, a cup of synthetic yogurt, vitamin-enriched water, and strong coffee. It wasn't bad, but it was boring. I would've killed for a fresh apple.

Kamal didn't seem to mind. He sat down across from me and tore into his food while I picked apart the wrap.

He pointed at my yogurt. "Are you going to eat that?"

"All yours. Receiving Team ready today?"

"That's why I'm fueling up," he replied between bites. "This process is liable to take all day. Might not get to eat again except for what's stashed in the control room."

I shook my head. "Does Nex-Yes really need a media relay that far out?"

Kamal shrugged, taking a spoonful of yogurt. "We'll be out there soon enough."

I downed my water, and wished him luck. Dropping off my tray, I left the cafeteria after refilling my coffee and headed off towards my own station in the Integrity bay. We had to watch over the data streams and ensure nothing got corrupted, lost, or gods forbid, hacked.

The latter had become less of a problem in the last ten years. By 2341, we had wiped out most of the radical anarchist groups in a joint venture with the other two conglomerates, Thur-Now and Dis-Viz. They had put an end to Word War IV in 2136 with money instead of bombs, securing their dominance, taking us out into the solar system only a few decades later.

Colonizing the entire system had been simple once the Big Three fell into a race to develop short-range jump technology, and figured out how to build miniature artificial suns. There were now forty-eight colonies stretching from the moon to a spot outside of Neptune, where we were currently floating. Each one was owned and operated by one of the conglomerates.

"Darcy, over here!" I heard when I walked into the bay.

I strolled over to a holo screen to see Kim squinting at the display. "What's up?"

"Big day. Elon-B is now 10 AU away from the Kuiper Belt, ready for data transfer."

"All alone in the black, broadcasting to absolutely nothing."

Kim shot me a look. "We don't know that. And Nex-Yes will have a colony out there in under a decade. We need to be ready before the other corporations beat us."

I tried not to roll my eyes. While I knew the conglomerates had done a great deal of good for humanity, I was also aware they had promoted a certain type of fascism. Zealotry made for greater productivity. Unfortunately for the Big Three, you could burn books back in the old days, but you couldn't burn data streams now, and nothing was ever really deleted.

Halfway back to my console, Gustav came into the bay. "Attention, everyone! You all know what today is. Receiving Team will be handling the input from Elon-B when it comes online, making sure it's functioning properly. Production Team already has the first packet ready and handed off to Shipping Team, who will upload. I know everyone is excited, but that packet is Alpha-Tentpole encoded."

Groans went up among those in the Integrity Team.

"I know, I know," Gustav said, holding up his hands. "Nex-Yes is concerned about security threats, hackers of all kinds of you catch my meaning. Even Kansas is on Orange Alert."

I raised an eyebrow. Our security A.I. droids were armed? It *was* conceivable that one of the other conglomerates could try to sneak in and pull some corporate espionage. Or worse, tank the project.

"Receiving Team will be monitoring the data stream until 15:00, then it's officially ours. Okay? We're Neptune-Yang Station, let's jump into it."

Kamal hadn't said a word. What a dick.

The clock counted down to 9:00 and there was a cheer in the Integrity bay when a message came up on main display announcing that Elon-B looked good. I have to admit, I felt a bit caught up in the giddiness of my coworkers. With renewed vigor, I dove into my work, scouring the streams for any irregularities with my cognitive mods. My neuralnet was plugged into my music library, so I didn't hear when Gustav came up behind me.

"Oh, sorry," I said, disconnecting. "I was in the deep."

He leaned in closer. "We haven't had an update from Receiving in three hours, not since the initial uplink."

"They're probably not used to doing their job *and* ours on top of it. You want me to go down?"

Gustav frowned. "I sent Kim an hour ago. She wouldn't shut up about going."

I almost laughed, but the look on his face stopped me. Kim would have gotten back to us by now. Beyond anything else, she was stickler for protocol.

"What do you want me to do, boss?" I asked.

Gustav scanned the bay, and I followed his gaze. As a Manager, he oversaw twenty-four Integrity Associates, including myself and Kim, who were both Deputy Mangers. Technically, it was against policy for him to leave the bay without calling in another Manager or one of the Assistant Managers.

"Listen up," he said. "I know it's against protocol, but we may have a problem. I'm going to check on a situation, and I'm leaving Deputy Manager Darcy Garza in charge. I should be right back."

As he left, one of the new recruits, whose name I couldn't remember, asked me if everything was alright. I decided to throw Kim under the bus and blame it on her. I went back to work, but didn't re-net my music. At this point, my unease was growing.

What came first was the stench.

It was sweet, almost honey-like, but with rancid undertones. Something rotting. I pulled myself away from the holo screen and looked around the room. Everyone had noticed it. The idea that it might be food gone bad was nearly inconceivable. Ninety percent of our consumables were processed synthetics, plus nothing could turn that quickly.

"Did somebody just shit in a wastebasket?" asked Duggan.

"No," said Ravi. "That's decay. The smell of death."

One of the team went over to the door to peer out down the corridor and gave a shriek, jumping back. She scurried over to Ravi, hiding behind him.

"What is it?" I asked.

She said nothing, eyes wide.

Grumbling, I climbed out of my seat and made my way over to the door. Honestly, I didn't want to cross that threshold, but everyone behind me was watching, waiting. Everything directly outside looked normal, and a glance to my right revealed nothing out of the ordinary. Then I turned left and almost screamed.

The walls were covered in insects. No, the walls were *made* of insects. They were shifting and transforming, living planes that took on new dimensions beyond what I understood. Bugs didn't *exist* on the space station; walls obeyed the laws of physics here. Instead, the stench knocked me back as holes began to appear between the titling, undulating patterns. Not holes into space, but gaps into reality, voids that were a Deeper Black. Instead of emptiness, it was teeming.

I fell back into the bay hyperventilating. Ravi and another of my teammates were by my side, the young woman who had already looked out desperately trying to hail someone from Higher Management. Another had already tried to summon one of Kansas's security droids. Duggan went to step out, but I grabbed his leg and yanked him back.

He pulled free and stepped into the hallway. I watched his face as it went from confusion, to horror, into madness. He stumbled headlong right into whatever insanity awaited him down there.

"We can't stay here," I said, getting to my feet.

One of the other new recruits wrung his hands. "But there are protocols to follow!"

"Fuck protocols! Reality is being torn apart by insects out there!"

"I'm not leaving this room," said the young woman who had also witnessed what I had.

While I could understand her terror, I couldn't understand the rest of the team. Most of them wouldn't leave out of sheer blind obedience to Nex-Yes. A woman named Alice agreed to leave with me along with Ravi. I was pretty sure Ravi had seen some of his own horrors back on the Mars revolt as a child.

As we were leaving, an older man known among the staff

as an outspoken corporatist tried to stop us. "You'll lose all your credit and be listed as unemployable. Unemployable!"

"Maybe, but we'll be alive," I said.

He spat, actually spat, on the ground. "Better buried than carried!"

A "carrier," was someone who didn't work for a conglomerate. A stupid slur, really. I understood the sentiment, but in this context, the denial was mind blowing.

I kneed the idiot in the groin and ushered the others out of the door, all of us careful to keep our eyes to the right.

We hurried down the corridor, past a number of maintenance terminals. I didn't want to risk glancing behind until we reached the bend ahead. Shortly past that was a T-Junction that would take us either to the cafeteria or hydroponics.

"Keep moving," said Ravi.

At the junction, I slowly turned my head, expecting nightmares. Nothing.

"Now where?" asked Alice.

"Let's try the cafeteria."

That was a mistake.

The cafeteria was filled with what appeared to be purplish-black vines enveloping the floor, walls, and ceiling. They had grown over the tables and chairs, absorbing parts of the food that had been set out on the trays. Worse, illuminated by the few lights that still flickered above, they had begun to grow through the dozen or so people present in the room.

One person sat in a chair, unaffected off to the side of the room.

I took a hesitant step into the cafeteria. "Gustav?"

"So inquisitive, so confident," he said, he voice raw like he'd been screaming.

"Gustav, what happened?" I asked, afraid to get much closer. "Was it Elon-B? Something in the data stream?"

"Conquest, order, definitions," he said. "There are no definitions, simply the entropic. A never-ending multitude."

Ravi pulled at my hand. "We need to go."

I went to open my mouth, but as I did, so did Gustav. And it kept opening. The jaw extended far past what it should have been able to naturally, and what looked like small, spindly arms reached out of his mouth. Rising to his feet, his limbs thinned and lengthened, then took two wobbly steps towards us.

We didn't wait around to watch him take anymore.

Back at the junction, the insects had progressed, and Alice screamed when she saw what was becoming of the space station. Ravi dragged her along and we did our best to scramble onwards to the hydroponics bay. I was terrified it had already been compromised, but it seemed untouched. We moved a few supply containers in front of door once we were inside. It wasn't about to keep anything out, but it made us feel better. Once we had the illusion of safety, we collapsed and tried to sort out our next move.

Alice held her face in her hands. "What the hell is going on?"

"This has to be Elon-B," said Ravi. "Can't be a coincidence."

I agreed. "All I can think is that something hijacked the data stream when that initial input was coming back in to Receiving."

"Something?"

I rubbed my temples. "Yes, something. We're not dealing with Big Three bullshit here. This is legitimately…"

"Alien," Alice finished.

"Yeah."

"Well," said Ravi, "It was theorized we'd have to move beyond our solar system before anyone out there would pay attention to us. I just didn't think it would be like this."

I pulled a stim out my pocket and popped it in my mouth. "We deluded ourselves into expecting starships and diplomacy, intergalactic councils and trade negotiations. War at the worst, profits at the best."

"Isn't *this* an act of war?" asked Alice.

"No. This is someone playing with their food."

There was some argument on what to do next. Ravi and Alice wanted to go out the side door as soon as possible, but I wanted to get a better grip on our situation first. If whatever this was had slipped into the station via Elon-B's data stream, I had to wonder how much of it was affecting our neuralnets. Had anything I'd seen in the hallway or cafeteria been real, or just hallucinations brought on from some sort of malware? None of us had been jacked in during work, the whole point of what we did in Integrity counted on us being stream-free, but that didn't mean we still weren't compromised in some way. Alice seemed convinced of this, it being far more likely than nihilistic space gods. Still, I cautioned against any of us activating our own ID networks until we found more staff.

Ravi didn't seem to side with Alice or me. As far as he was concerned, while the cafeteria might be explainable, the hallway wasn't. That had defied logic. It wasn't just a matter of some special effects zapped into our brains, it had transcended our understanding of sciences. He delved into some things I didn't fully understand. He said that while the hallway could still be there in theory, we had witnessed the foundations our universe being dismantled by higher properties.

While we were busy having a theoretical debate on the nature of the reality like a bunch of assholes, the side door slid open. I managed to choke back a scream, expecting the worst. It took a few seconds for me to register it was Kansas, our security A.I., inhabiting one of his many Android bodies. We all rushed to him, only to see him stagger and fall into a row of planters.

Ravi held us back before we got too close, the nutrient crystals spilling out over Kansas as he lay there. His white, polymer skin had somehow been cracked in a few spots, even discolored in a manner that would have suggested blemishes on a human. Neon blue eyes rolled around in his skull blindly as a small shudder afflicted parts of his body.

"Kansas, what happened?" asked Ravi.

The android's voice crackled and squawked. "Systemic – could not predict the – my quantum – last unit in my security division – sixty-eight percent of Yang Station."

One of his eyes went dark as I leaned forward. "Kansas, please! What's going on?"

The android seemed to focus on my voice. "Incursion is macro-spatial – All information is rewritable."

The other eye went dark.

I tried not to think about what Kansas had told us as we snuck out of hydroponics, but it had terrified me. This was way too big to try and wrap my head around, any attempt leaving me wanting to curl up in a ball. Instead, I followed Ravi towards the shuttle bay. It was only by sheer luck that he was a certified pilot. The idea of braving the black in a life pod was almost worse than what was happening on the station. Almost.

We saw more of those vines in the main corridor and had to backtrack. Fortunately, Nex-Yes had money to blow and had built redundancies on top of the redundancies. Down another hallway, but we didn't make it far before that smell smacked us in the face. I risked a peek around the bend and saw the swirling, morphing tunnel of insects. Holding back my vomit, we ran the other direction.

"Now what?" asked Alice.

"We go up," replied Ravi, pointing to a utility ladder.

I unzipped my navy blue uniform jacket and dropped it to the ground. Protocol didn't matter much at this point, although Alice side eyed my non-regulation tank top with a cartoon character on it. I retied my blonde hair back into a tighter ponytail and followed Ravi.

We had seen some undoubtedly weird and horrific things, but I had to wonder about the bugs and the vines. They seemed to be the two themes most common on the station. If what Kansas had said was even half correct, I could only guess at their purpose.

The ladder scaled, we bolted down the hall that would take us closer to the shuttle bay. The lights in this corridor were mostly out, and I whispered for Ravi to slow down. I didn't want us to accidentally go running into anything lurking in the shadows. There was a dim illumination ahead, and that somehow bothered me more than the darkness. It felt like a harbinger of bad things to come, and dread began to clamp down on my bones. It didn't help that as we drew nearer, we heard soft chanting, a litany of nonsense words.

Alice didn't share my terror. "Survivors!"

She ran ahead before either Ravi or I could stop her. We chased after as she skidded short right inside what had once been the Production bay. A number of small fires had been started, the room's extinguishers rigged so that they wouldn't go off. The flames danced in wastebaskets and desk drawers, revealing eight or so staff members on their knees reciting the babble. Before them, on a large wall, was a messy patina of every bodily fluid imaginable. No symbol, no picture, just smears and splatter. It appeared as if it had been caked on there for years.

"What... what the fuck?" Alice managed to get out.

Without missing a beat in their prayers, the staff rose from their knees and turned. I don't fully understand what had happened to them, but they had changed. Not only had they all aged over thirty years, perhaps forty, they had all become ravaged by some sort of mutagenic virus. Their wrinkled flesh was twisted into unspeakable forms, coated in seeping lesions and ripe boils, while their graying hair was parted by unnatural protrusions and growths. Their uniforms were in tatters, one only still wearing socks.

Despite their advanced age and misshaped bodies, they were on Alice like lightning.

With their voices raised to a frenzied pitch, they all began clawing, thrusting, and biting. Alice wailed as she was torn apart, only for the staff to begin spitting blood on her battered form. Some broke open their sores and allowed pus to drain into her wounds.

Alice's eyes caught mine, screaming as her skin began to bubble.

I was a coward. I ran, and Ravi followed me.

We got back to the ladder and fled up another level. This would be the top level of the shuttle bay, so we'd have to make it from here. We didn't have any other options or choices left

I was breathing hard, trying to process what had just happened. All my nerves were keyed up. I though about dropping into my neuralnet and trying to adjust some settings, but I didn't trust any of my mods at this point. I didn't trust anything.

Just as I was thinking that, Ravi touched my elbow. I jumped, ready to hit him. He held up his hands, taking a step back. It was obvious he was just as scared as I was.

"I'm sorry. I'm just having a real hard time here," I whispered.

"I know, me too. That was Yusef back there. I play racket games with him twice a week."

"I thought I had a handle on this. I was obviously full of shit."

"I've been thinking about what that Gustav creature said. He used the word 'entropic.' Do you know what that is?"

"It's like chaos, right?"

Ravi smiled. "It's the process of order to disorder, often through destruction or consumption. Think about what we've seen, eh? Insects, vines, and now disease."

"And religion," I added.

"I'm not sure about that last one, but we won't argue theology. Still, if an alien intelligence wanted to torment us with this abstract concept, it would need to know what humans consider, well, chaotic and destructive forces."

"Why not just come at us with war and death?"

Ravi shrugged. "Who knows. I'm not a hyper-dimensional entity from beyond the stars. Why is it doing any of this?"

Annoyed, I took off down the corridor. At this point, I didn't care anymore about the why or what or how, I simply wanted off Neptune-Yang. I didn't care if I was listed as a "carrier," as long as I survived this. Whatever was happening here wasn't as cut and dry as contracting RIKS or accidentally getting blown out an airlock. There you died, end of story. Something told me death wasn't the end of your suffering here.

Nothing delayed our progress to the shuttle bay, but sounds followed our step. Crashes and groans, creaks and screams. Others noises that couldn't be identified. The door opened up to the massive hanger revealing all the pods still present and only one shuttle gone. I didn't know whether to be elated or distraught. We had our pick, but that meant very few had escaped so far.

Ravi and I agreed not to risk using one of the elevators for various reasons, and braved the long climb down. He went first, taking the ladder in expert fashion. It occurred to me I was going to have to ask him about his youth on Mars during our long trek back. It would be almost a week to Saturn by shuttle.

I was almost down when I heard Ravi scream. "Jump! Left!"

I did as I was told even though I was still too high up. I landed hard, bouncing off a stack of fuel rods, pain shooting up my leg. Spinning on my side, I brought my head up to the bottom of the ladder and let out a wail.

The bottom of the ladder was gone. The wall was gone. It was nothing but a squirming mass of insects.

We hadn't been able to see it from above, but the whole lower wall of the shuttle bay had lost cohesion to the infestation. Its existence shifted and skittered, the three-dimensional plane slanting into the awaiting maw of a greater darkness that lay hidden beneath space.

Ravi floated in the wall, half-consumed by it. He was screaming, but no sound was able to reach me. Then he was hurled down into that Deeper Black.

Lurching away on a broken ankle, I wept as I made my way towards a life pod. I couldn't fly a shuttle. No idea how to.

Somehow I got across the bay and slammed my palm against the emergency activation panel. At that point, part of me didn't expect it to work, but the pod door opened and I pulled myself in. Pulling the straps over me, I thought I saw someone in the shuttle bay, as I punched all the buttons to prepare for launch.

I went rigid as a voice came over the intercom saying my name. "Darcy Keyes Garza."

It was Kamal's voice.

"So feeble, so limited. Such small pursuits."

I struggled against the fear to get the last codes in place.

"We are the engines of entropy, the immolation swarm. We are the long black room, and you have always been inside us."

The pod readied itself and the countdown began. It was only a five second one, but that was far too long. An eternity. In that time, I saw the shape from across the shuttle bay come closer.

What I thought had been a shadow was wrong. Vaguely humanoid, with the proportions drastically off, like a child's drawing. It was a hole in reality. Occupying more than three dimensions, it affected the space around it as it moved. Cargo decayed, rusted, and fell apart. Other items were sucked into its event horizon, vanishing from existence.

The pod blasted out of the station and into the black.

I'm now floating out here, in a synchronous orbit around Saturn. Under normal circumstances, I'd use my neuralnet to link up with a data stream and call for help, but I'm terrified of what could happen. There's no way to know how corrupted the streams are, how far that influence has reached. I've recorded this all in my own private log so at least if I don't survive, hopefully a good data retrieval team can deep dive for it. I'll be activating cryo-sleep here shortly.

The stars used to bring me peace, but not anymore. Looking out through this tiny hatch, all I can think about are the last words it said. Now, I see them between the stars.

I can only hope I awaken to a system still alive, that someone is out there to hear me. Then I remember what I said to Kim this morning when it all began, "All alone in the black, broadcasting to absolutely nothing."

3

BLIGHT ON YOUR TONGUE

THERE WERE FAR MORE people than Howe had expected. They estimated close to three thousand in the initial briefing, but a number of others in the security detail didn't think the project would pull in nearly close to that count. Howe had agreed with them, and now been proven wrong.

The corridor was filled with technicians scurrying about, seeing to last minute details. A lot of panels never got covered, exposed wires and pipes everywhere. He dodged a squirrelly looking man mumbling to himself while he gawked at a data tablet. A team of men hauled a length of cable as thick as an arm down a set of stairs to hook it up on a lower floor. You could tell their stress levels were through the roof.

Howe stepped past a few more people, including a thin woman screaming at two electricians. They didn't even notice as he squeezed by, which said something. In his experience, most people had a tendency to glance at a six-foot-three black man loaded down with weapons.

Pressing his thumb on the access pad, he waited for his biometrics to be read and the door to open. Immediately, the scent of the jungle hit him. Even with all of the construction done in the surrounding area, you could still smell it. Howe walked out onto the fourth level catwalk, what everyone called a rim, and peered out.

They were somewhere in Columbia, but even he wasn't sure of their exact coordinates. All the supplies had come in by boat from the west, everyone flown in later. The whole project had been incredibly under the radar, or as best as The Affiliates could pull off. Nicknamed "The Stadium," its entire construction had been pulled off in under four months. Standing on one of its outer rims now, so close to the end goal, Howe just wanted to go home.

"Hey fuck face, you pissing off the edge?"

Howe sighed and turned. Lopez sauntered up, that stupid grin on his face. He was in the same dark gray uniform with the Blockade Security insignia emblazoned on the shoulder. Through some disturbing twists, he had achieved a captain ranking the same as Howe.

"How's the perimeter look?" asked Howe.

"Think we got more protestors heading our way, but they'll get the welcoming committee if they show."

Howe grit his teeth but said nothing.

Lopez fiddled with his gun, oblivious to Howe's discomfort. "Hey, did you hear? In another hour Bale will lose all executive authority to Nobel."

"I'm sure she's thrilled about that."

Lopez shrugged. "We still have operational control, but that doctor will be in charge of The Stadium. El hombres es un cientîficio loco. For real."

"The world belongs to the mad scientists now, Lopez. Soldiers like us are just kept around for show."

Lopez didn't like that, and wandered off grumbling. It was true, though. The world's near brush with World War III in 2028 proved that. Men with guns were nothing compared to a hacker with some disinformation. One guy pressing his enter key in his basement could do more damage in an instant than a platoon could every hope to do with all their bullets in a day. It was a sobering realization that made a lot of folks rethink certain strategies.

Howe continued his walk along the fourth level rim. From here he had a good view of the area, mostly just greenery in the distance. A few transport vehicles parked nearby and a number of outbuildings housing supplies. The sun would be dipping behind the horizon in another couple of hours, and later tonight everything would kick off.

The Imago Project. It was silly bullshit as far as he was concerned, but The Affiliates had dropped billions on it. They had built this place in the middle of nowhere just to achieve their goal. After the way things had been going the last ten years, people jumped at the chance to help them.

Howe fingered the M27-Q automatic rifle strapped to his chest. It was state of the art, nothing like he would have had as a private back in 2028, when the world almost went to war. Hackers, both sanctioned and unsanctioned, had whipped extremist factions all across the world into a frenzy. Militia groups, terrorist organizations, rightwing hardliners, religious sects, and hatemongers were all pushed into action. Worse, most governments were crippled, or else steered into debilitating debts.

The world almost collapsed and we never did find out why. Many of the individuals behind the cyber attacks were found, but most died before questioning. All of that effort, all of that chaos, and it was rendered pointless.

Over a dozen multi-national corporations stepped in. They cleaned up the mess, took out the hackers with security forces like Blockade, and stabilized the globe again in a matter of two months. The people were thrilled, but the governments less so, especially after the corporations consolidated as The Affiliates. While they openly said they were more concerned about profit loss than human life, many thought it might be more than that.

Howe had heard the rumor that The Affiliates organized

the 2028 hacks to begin with so they could swoop in and save the day. He wouldn't be surprised, but in the end, he didn't care. It was now 2039, over a decade later, and he was a thirty-year-old man. He could remember being a teenager in high school, being fifteen and seeing girls crying in terror at the thought of a militia attack. Fear like that didn't exist anymore, and he was willing to accept the price.

Most of the time.

Rounding the rim, he saw that protestors had indeed found their way to The Stadium. Howe was still baffled how they knew about this place, let alone how to find it. It was a small group, maybe twenty in all. Lead by a scruffy young man with long hair, they all carried hastily constructed signs with slogans like "People Not Profits," and "Humans > Companies." He didn't disagree with them, but they didn't seem to realize what they had walked into.

Below, Lopez strolled out with a squad of Blockade Security. "You're all trespassing on Affiliate property!"

"You've stolen this land from the Columbian people!" the man shouted back. "Now you're raping it for your evil, capitalist endeavors!"

Lopez laughed. "This land was bought for half a billion dollars. And do you even know what is happening here?"

The man tried to sputter out a response, but Lopez waived away his response. "Doesn't matter, jefe. You're on our land and you're in Columbia now."

"Wait, wait!" the man squealed as the squad raised their rifles.

The entire group of protestors were dropped in a barrage of bullets. Howe closed his eyes and gripped the railing. He understood no protestor could be allowed to leave, to get any word of the project back to the outside, but killing them seemed a bit much. Director Bale said they barely had enough supplies to provide to the technicians, the security, and all the participants, and no one was going to go hungry because a few hippies wanted to disrupt the show. He supposed it made sense, but it didn't make him happy.

The squad began to drag the bodies over to one of the outbuildings, specifically designated for corpses. They hadn't anticipated so many protestors, so the structure was already filling up. At their last daily briefing, there were about one hundred and twenty protestors in there, not to mention the sixty-some people who had died during construction on The Stadium. At this point, it would either become a mass grave, or more likely a very large bonfire.

Howe had seen enough for the day. He headed back, taking in the green vista with the dying light. You didn't see anything like this in Indiana, definitely not these lush mountains. It really was beautiful here. Not too hot either, somewhere in the high seventies. Nice when you were in full gear. He had been in places where all you did was sweat. Columbia wasn't the reason he was ready to go home, it was Blockade.

Tossing that idea around, he up stopped short when he passed another door on the rim and found a young white woman smoking a cigarette. She was gorgeous, with her dark hair pulled up in a ponytail. All she had on was one of those sheer black robes the participants wore, revealing her body. Howe tried to pull his eyes away from the curves on her petite frame.

"Uh…" said Howe, deciding the mountains were a safer place to look.

"Shit, I just lit this up."

Howe's eyes found the pack in her hand. "Wait, are those real cigarettes?"

"Maybe."

"Girl, how did you get those, and how can I get one?"

She grinned. "The local crew used to smuggle them in. I traded my handheld PS14 for a carton. I'll give you one if you don't bust me."

"Deal."

She handed him one and he lit it up. Howe hadn't had real tobacco in years, the synthetic stuff was fine but never really the same. A little groan escaped him as he exhaled.

"I know, right?" she said.

"I'm Caleb Howe."

"Vivian Bette."

"Vivian, how did you manage to get this door open?"

"I double majored in computer science and mechanical engineering."

"Yeah, that'll fucking do it."

Vivian laughed. "I'm surprised you haven't seen me before. I've been running around here as I pleased since I arrived three weeks ago. Hell, Dr. Nobel tried to pull me off participant and give me a job."

"I was just going to ask that. You seem qualified enough."

Vivian took a puff off her smoke and stared out at the growing darkness. "My big brother Victor. He was my hero. Victor and Vivian, V and V. He went in for a basic medical procedure, nothing dangerous. That was back in '27."

Howe leaned on the railing. "The big med hack."

"Hundreds of thousands died, but only one that mattered to me. Sure, some things have changed since then, but it hasn't been enough. We need something fundamentally new."

Howe raised an eyebrow. "And you think that's going to happen with Project Imago?"

"I don't know, but if so, I want to help however I can."

He nodded. Howe wished he had her outlook, her passion to do good.

"What about you?" Vivian asked. "Just like guns?"

Howe snorted. "I was a nineteen year old private who narrowly missed dying in a pointless war back in '28. I did my time then joined Blockade to help The Affiliate because I felt like they saved me. But I've seen just as many horrors since then. I wasn't saved. I feel like it's just too... I'm not even sure."

Vivian stubbed out her cigarette and flicked the butt over the railing. Handing the half empty pack to Howe, she surprised him by getting up on her tiptoes and kissing him quickly on the lips.

"Keep the smokes. I'm glad I got to spend time with you before the ritual. You're going to find your way, Caleb Howe. The only way is forward."

She gave his hands another squeeze and disappeared through the door, her robe briefly fluttering open. Howe realized he had been holding his breath, and let it go. He hadn't even said goodbye. There was a very good chance he would never see her again.

"I hope you survive tonight, Vivian Bette," he said to night air.

ABOUT AN HOUR LATER, Howe ran into Lopez again. With no one else really to talk to, he thought about telling his co-captain about Vivian. Unfortunately Lopez was too riled up about the prospect of more incoming protestors.

"We gotta have a leak, that's the only answer," said Lopez.

Howe shrugged. "Who cares? In a few more hours this will be all over."

Lopez spun on him. "Some penqueña perra es disloyal, yo! Disrespecting us? Fuck no!"

Suppressing the urge to roll his eyes, Howe walked away. Lopez had some weird obsession with respect. One of his men, Vasquez, had told him that Lopez once tried to pass off that he had been part of the cartels in Southern California. Vasquez hadn't bought it and went snooping in the personnel files. The sociopathic captain had grown up in a very pleasant suburb outside of San Francisco.

He supposed they all had their reasons for being here.

One technician was nearly in tears, her fingers bleeding as

she finished some last minute wiring. Everyone inside the walls of The Stadium was manic, attempting to complete final details before things kicked off at four a.m.. Thousands of participants waited in their rooms beneath, tiny spaces little more than cells, seeing to whatever preparations they needed. Howe hadn't read upmuch about that aspect of the project; what he did know seemed highly dubious.

His comms chirped, telling him to double-time it to the command center. Worried there may have been another incident like last month, he gripped his rifle close to his chest and barreled down the hall. People were smart enough to get out of his way this time.

He made it up two floors and a third a way around the Stadium in under a minute. Barely out of breath, he swept past two armed guards at the door and surveyed the observation room. Nothing appeared amiss.

The room was long and narrow, dimly lit, and filled with an array of half-life quantum computers, sliver light monitors, holo-data relays, live biometric scanners, and telemetry equipment of every type. Half a billion dollars just in one room. A few of the white hats gawked at him, but quickly turned back to their keyboards.

"Howe, over here."

Turning, he found Director Bale looking over a digital map. She was still a striking a woman in her late forties – tall, lean, and angular. Something about her short black hair and dark eyes reminded Howe of a raven.

"There has been a… compromise between your Commander and Nobel. There won't be any security on the field, but I'm assigning twenty to the first floor alcoves. You'll be in charge of those men."

Howe didn't like hearing this, especially when it wasn't coming from Royce. He chewed on his words for a moment before answering. "I'll go where I'm needed ma'am, but may I ask where Commander Royce is now?"

"I assume on the first floor."

Howe nodded and stood there. Bale eventually realized he was still there and dismissed him. As he was leaving, she called out his name.

"Howe, no matter what happens, you are not to step foot on the field. Do you understand?"

"Yes, ma'am."

Finding his way to the lower floor, he began to wonder what exactly this project was all about. As far as he had been lead to believe, The Affiliates had dropped a bunch of money on some mystical nonsense to get a leg up on the governments. There were whispers that some kind of massive gladiatorial match would be involved, the participants forced to fight each other. How that would lead to some magical mumbo-jumbo, he didn't know.

The first floor was relatively quiet compared to higher ones. Stepping out onto the interior rim, Howe could see the field. It was approximately sixty-four thousand square feet round, a little larger than an American football field. Take out the actual seating, and you could see why they called it The Stadium. Of course, the field was nothing but bare dirt, and a bizarre statue had been erected in the center.

Royce spotted him and marched over in his direction. The Commander looked more grizzled than usual. Slender and graying, his skeletal façade belied a strength men half his age would kill to possess. At the moment, a lot of that vigour looked sapped.

"You talk to Bale?" asked Royce.

"Yes, sir."

"Noble is a fucking lunatic and I don't know why that woman is going along with his blatant lunacy."

"She didn't seem real happy about it, sir."

Royce nodded absently, peering down at the field. "Ayup, have to agree with that."

"Bale told me not to step foot on the floor under any circumstances. What are your orders, sir?"

Royce chuckled. "You stay on the first, let it all play out. Even if it's sus. Only engage if events threaten to spill off the field. If someone wants to shit talk that call, I'll cover it."

"Understood, sir."

"You've heard about what's going to go down here tonight?"

"Heard some rumors, sir. I don't pay much mind to gossip."

Royce glanced back out to the field. "It's going to be worse."

AROUND ELEVEN THAT NIGHT, Howe went and caught some rack time. Only two hours, but it was enough. There was no way he could've slept any longer even if he would've wanted to. He lay there and ran his hands across his head, staring at the ceiling. So many whispers about this night for weeks now, Howe just wanted it over with. He pulled himself out of bed, got dressed, and tried not to think about Vivian.

The Stadium was buzzing with anticipation. Out of the nearly three thousand people there, about two-thirds of them were participants waiting down in their rooms. The remaining thousand were comprised of technicians, operators, administrators, and security, the last only a unit of one hundred and twenty. It had turned out that minus the protestors, Blockade hadn't really been needed. Many who had worked on the project were exciting to see it come to fruition, and some just wanted to see what all the fuss had been about.

At two a.m., Commander Royce once again met with his captains, Howe and Lopez, going over the plans. Howe was stationed inside, on the inner first rim, and Lopez had the outside perimeter. The five team leaders were briefed, and told to disseminate assignments to their squads.

As everyone broke to check their gear, Royce slid up next to him. "Remember, stay off the field unless shit tries to creep up onto the rim."

Howe frowned. "Of course, sir."

"It's gonna get weird, son."

Before Howe could respond, his commander walked away. That statement worried him more than anything else he had heard so far in his time at The Stadium.

The security force spent the next hour checking all their equipment. Along with his M27-Q, he also had a Sig Sauer V779, which had been made exclusively for Blockade. The nine-millimeter semi-automatic pistol was smaller yet had greater stopping power than it's previous iterations. A handful of his heavies carried M240-IO's, next-gen machine guns that were belt fed with tracker rounds. All this along with ballistic body armor, ammunition pouches, stun grenades, fragmentation grenades, flares, thermal and night vision goggles, k-bar, tactical taser, and a digital servant synced up to the comm system. The gear specs had been specifically drawn up for this mission, so things like med kits had been left out in favour of more ammo – there were literally over one hundred doctors running about the place, after all.

Despite their reasoning, Howe was still a little salty about that.

The hour fast approaching, everyone scrambled to positions. Many would be watching from stations throughout The Stadium, ensuring the numbers. The science was way above Howe's head, if there was even any science involved here. It all had to do with digital synesthesia and gestalt consciousness. When he had heard one physicist raving on about how this could result in a quantum sympathectomy, he had stopped caring. It was all billionaires playing at sci-fi witch-craft as far as he could tell.

Howe took his spot and checked his watch. Almost time.

He really wished he had another one of those cigarettes.

AT SEVEN MINUTES after four a.m., the lights all went out inside the field. For a brief moment, there was only darkness. Then red orbs positioned all around the first rim began to pulse. Howe realized they were tuned to the pace of a human heart-beat. As his eyes adjusted, he saw the participants: one thou-sand, nine hundred and sixty-two people streaming out onto the field.

They were all naked except for those sheer black robes. All the participants had tied them tightly at the front ,with a belt that also secured two pouches at their hips. They moved with a sense of rhythm and purpose out from the lower quarters, and began to circle around the statue in the center.

The thing was hideous, in Howe's opinion. Some modern art piece that was vaguely humanoid, it had been constructed out of welded steel and stood twelve feet tall. Full of curves and negative space, it had been filled with all types of speak-ers, cameras, lights, and other devices. It looked even less like a piece of artwork now, more like some science fiction night-mare. He had no idea why it had been stuck there.

Or more importantly, why it had just lit up white; the throbbing bass had intensified.

The participants began to disrobe, their sheer garments discarded on the dirt. Howe realized there were chants coming from somewhere above him, but he couldn't place where. Real voices or recorded, the language was unrecogniz-able. Suddenly something like a gong rang out and a second, faster beat kicked in.

It was on. The almost two thousand participants began to

caress and kiss each other, skin finding skin. The moans grew louder as bodies slid against each other, inside each other. The red orbs continued to pulse slowly, revealing images of an orgy. A sea of flesh tasting and touching, thrusting and trembling. The scent of sex and sweat grew strong and the sounds became a roar. What had began as erotic, became something else to Howe, something nearly divine. A singular mass writhing in pleasure for eighteen minutes.

Then the klaxon when off.

It was less an alarm and more an aria, but it was loud and jarring. It also brought with it a change in the lights, the orbs now strobing. Before Howe could process much of this, he bore witness to how it affected the participants. They had entered the second phase of the ritual.

Those pouches on their belts had concealed small knives. Three-inch push daggers, but still very deadly, two for each. They scrambled for their weapons and began killing each other in religious furor. Without hesitation, they attacked those they had just been embracing. Blood sprayed through the air and spilled on the ground, bodies trampled underfoot. A different kind of scream filled The Stadium now. The daggers were used to slit throats, plunge into eyes, tear open bellies, and dismember genitalia. The field was awash in carnage.

Thoughdifficult to see, Howe could make out enough to stay with him forever. One man sat down and casually peeled the skin off the face of another participant, his victim still alive. Lying there between his assailant's crossed legs, he begged for death. Instead of release, he lost an ear. He was so engrossed in his work, skinning a face, he didn't notice someone run up behind him and shove a dagger into the back of his skull. Maybe they thought the guy in his lap was already dead, because he was left weeping.

Three young women chased down a middle-aged man and tackled him, stabbing him in the side as he went down.

He squealed as they rolled him over and proceeded to mutilate his genitals to red, wet mess. Force feeding him pieces of his butchered manhood, he coughed up blood and vomit. One of the girls grew angry and began stabbing him, which set off the other two. All three had an argument until they spied another potential target and bolted off.

What seemed to be a couple had cornered a woman against the wall. It looked like she was pleading with one of his squadmates to help her. Howe thought it was Wright, but he couldn't be sure. Gripping his M27-Q tighter, he watched to see how it would unfold, hoping he wouldn't have to intervene. Fortunately, the couple grew bored and just swooped in, both guys taking turns stabbing her.

Howe sighed. What was the point of all this?

That was when everything went stupid.

The lights and sounds began to turn strange. It was like they were made elastic, pliable and bent out of shape. Those photos you see of city highways at night, in slow motion, the lights stretched out like bright serpents: that's what was happening now. In some bizarre fashion, it was happening to the *sound* as well. Howe swore he could almost sense the screams moving in a singular direction instead of simply reverberating. It was all heading towards the statue.

Everyone stopped their murder orgy. They watched in awe as the light from the red orbs left with each strobe and glided on a trail to the center of the field. Every other light source did the same, leaving small glimmering streams. All sounds emitted would escape and somehow drift away, merging with the statue as the lights did. It was clear to anyone that whatever was happening, something there was growing in power.

Howe tapped comms. "Commander?"

"Steady everyone, this was expected. Do not engage. That's an order."

Howe raised an eyebrow. Obviously there was an entire

phase to the ritual the rank and file of Blockade didn't have clearance for.

The participants reacted in a number of different ways to the statue. Some backed away in fear, while others drew-closer. A few even knelt down in front of it, openly showing their devotion. Most seemed to have a healthy mix of wonder and distrust. A quick glance would estimate that two-thirds of those of the field were dead or dying.

Howe was about to radio Royce once more when the first corpse went flying through the air.

It was hard to make things out with the sound acting weird and all the streaming lights. He'd only seen movement and realized people were screaming. Then two more bodies went sailing up towards the statue. They went into the center mass and were simplyabsorbed. It was then Howe realized the darkness in the center of the statue was different, a deeper black. It was where all the light and sound had been going, now all the corpses too.

More bodies started being pulled up, dozens now. What was pretty before had become terrifying, although there were still a handful of devotees. The majority bailed towards the walls, to escape being bashed by a floating corpse if anything. The statue sucked in hundreds and the internal mechanical components that had been installed began to rearrange themselves.

The steel statue itself began to reshape as pieces of dead flesh fused to its internal structure, acting like an exoskeleton. All the technology that had been implanted inside it reconfigured as internal organs that floated in that dark energy. The red lights ran throughout it almost like a circulatory system. A cacophony of whispers, moans, screams, and others voices shook the field.

Then it took a step forward.

Still, some stayed at its feet, heads bowed. All the rest of the participants beat at the walls to be let out. The statue creature was no longer absorbing sound it seemed, but light was still bheaving weirdly around it. Howe flipped around his automatic rifle and trained it on the thing as it took another step. There was no way to know what was going to happen next.

A series of doors open. Most of the participants tried to flee, but found themselves at the end of a gun barrel. Howe sneered when he saw Dr. Nobel stroll in with his Genguard Unit. The only person on the project with separate security, those thugs of his would shoot babies for fun.

Surprisingly, once Noble was well out into the Field, he gestured for the participants to leave. Most happily took off, only a few dozen sticking around to see what came next. Ignoring the zealots still prostrated before the animated statue, he took a stance before it.

"Welcome!" said Noble. "Welcome to your birth. I am your creator, Dr. Dean Nobel. We have done so much to bring you here. You are The Imago God, The Divine Simulacrum. With you on our side, we shall pave a new way for humanity! It will be glorious, don't you think?"

What might have been a triangle of three white lights came alive in the center of its black headspace.

"Imago God," it repeated in Noble's voice.

"Yes!" said Nobel, bobbing his head excitedly.

Those three lights, which may have been eyes, burned brighter.

The words "Imago God" roared down at Noble in such a way that it stripped the flesh clean off his bones. The two Genguards next to him were taken out as well. The rest began to fire, but a series of lights and sounds began to emanate from The Imago God, decimating them. Two of Howe's men began to fire but static crackled across comms.

"Do not fire!" screamed Director Bale. "It's contained in the field!"

Howe leaned over the railing of the rim to see the doors

closing. Sure enough, all the participants had booked it out except seven remaining nutcases. Doors, Bale thought *doors* would hold this thing.

Howe hit comms. "Commander, where are you?"

"Going to see Bale."

"I'll meet you there."

<hr>

THE STADIUM HAD FALLEN into chaos. People were running about screaming, some hiding, and many fleeing into the jungle. The fact that so many were naked and covered in blood made it even more surreal. Some of the technicians struggled to keep at their job, while others simply gave up. Sprinting through the building, Howe saw a participant begging one of the Blockade Security force to shoot them before he was taken by The Imago God. Without time to intervene, he kept going.

Higher up, he found other participants having sex in the halls, while others resorting to more brutal outlets for their primal instincts. There were blood smears on the walls. The hall stank of offal. A beautiful girl, who couldn't have been any more than eighteen, sauntered naked through the corridors with entrails wrapped around her head like a scarf. Howe tried to banish that beaming smile she wore as he took the next set of stairs.

He heard the fighting before he found it. Rounding the corner, he saw a half dozen members of Blockade attempting to hold off a wave of people, all of them desperate to get into the command center for some reason. Maybe they thought it was safe in there, maybe they thought there was a secret way out. Maybe they just wanted to kill the people behind all this.

Howe was about to wade in when he heard the order given. He dropped just in time as bullets were released, cutting down almost the sixty or seventy that had assembled.

More senseless killing. Bodies fell on him, literal deadweight as he laid there. Blood soaked his uniform, slick and warm. Starting to push himself up, two of his men yelled something he didn't make out.

"If anyone shoots me, I'm going to be very pissed."

Realizing it was their captain lying among the dead, they scurried forward and pulled him lose. Scowling, he pried himself free and marched inside those precious doors they had been guarding. Here, everything was still pristine and calm.

Royce turned to him, eyes wide. "What the wild blue fuck happened to you?"

"I got caught in that cute little kill squad outside. Your order I'm guessing, Director Bale?"

She stood, arms folded, as though he had rudely interrupted a corporate meeting.

Bale raised an eyebrow. "Of course it was, we need to be in control of the situation. And I don't appreciate the tone, captain."

"Have you taken a look outside? You are far from in control."

"Nonsense," she replied with a wave of her hand. "The participants and the staff have done their jobs. We got what we wanted, and I don't care what they do now as long as they don't endanger the project."

Howe stared at her. "What exactly was the project? You can't expect us to do our job if we don't have the proper intel. Not on something like this."

Bale opened her mouth, then stopped. She glanced at Royce, who only gave her a shrug. She muttered something and stomped over to a holo desk.

"The last ten years has been a cold war of disinformation between the Affiliates and the governments. It's a battle of money and resources for dominance over the people. We realized a long time ago that waging straight out land assaults in the twenty-first century is costly and ineffective."

Howe clicked his tongue. "Yeah, one hacker is more powerful than a platoon of soldiers. I've heard that one, thanks."

"And you know what's more powerful that a team of hackers? An idea. You can't kill an idea. When thousands of people passionately get behind an idea, it becomes a belief. And if you weaponize a belief, it becomes a religion."

Howe's jaw dropped. They couldn't be that insane.

"The governments all have their own little patriotisms, their own faiths. It was the one thing the Affiliates didn't have, something people could think on in dark times. Well, we do now, and we brought it into reality. An artificial god. It's going to need a better name than what Nobel gave it, but marketing is looking into it."

The entire room shook, and Royce glanced out the window. "For the record, I think you're batshit crazy."

"Your unwanted opinion is dully noted."

"I agree with my Commander," said Howe. "Your Imago God doesn't seem terribly happy. How exactly do you plan on controlling it? If that's not classified?"

Bale sighed. "It is, but I can say that it's confined for now."

"By some walls?"

"By what amounts to a spiritual Faraday Cage. It traps the energy used to create it."

Royce had moved closer to the window. "Yeah, about that…"

Bale and Howe went over towards him just as alarms began to go off. The peered down into the field to see The Imago God absorbing the machinery in one corner that was used to trap it. Energy began to bend throughout the room, the very image of the field taking on skewed proportions. Howe covered his ears and went to one knee as a high-pitch wailing filled the command center.

The bending machinery snapped.

Part of the roof started to collapse. An entire section of the floor gave way at the same time, and Howe watched as Royce scrabbled to his feet. The older man looked dazed, but their eyes met for one brief moment. He lunged to grab his commander as a chunk of the ceiling came down and bashed him in the head. He was swept away with a massive portion of the command center. Sparks ignited a fire, and someone howled in pain. Leaping back, Howe raced out of room as it toppled out and fell piece by piece into the field.

Coughing from all the smoke that billowed out into the hall, he found only two staff members had made it along with two Blockade security members that had still been guarding the entrance. Bale had survived as well. She looked more pissed than anything else.

"You're ranking officer now, correct?"

"I guess, why?"

"I need you to escort me to…"

Howe shook his head. "No."

"Excuse me, Captain Howe?"

"Royce is dead. You're a fucking monster. I quit. I'm going to go try and save some people from that other monster."

Bale's face twisted up in a snarl. "You're supposed to do as you're told, don't you get that you fucking primate? A dumb soldier with a boomstick that obeys its betters. Now you best obey!"

Howe laughed, the other two Blockade security members chuckling with him. "Cute. You rich executive types really don't have a clue how the real world works, do you?"

He walked away, leaving her screeching as the two staff members tried to placate her. His two men walked with him, both grinning. He glanced over and saw their names were Shaffer and Stewart.

"You didn't have to come with me," said Howe.

"Fuck her," said Shaffer.

Stewart nodded. "We got your back, Captain. What's the play?"

Howe checked his gun. "We help."

They ran back down the stairs and looped around towards where it looked like the Imago God had broken through. A lot of people had already escaped and Howe estimated there were probably only a few hundred left in The Stadium. Still too many, but a lot better than three thousand.

Coming around a bend, they found a handful of people shuffling towards them. They all looked badly injured, two of them horribly burnt. Most of them appeared to be participants and flinched in fear when they saw the Blockade trio.

"Please don't hurt us!" one of them said.

"Why would we hurt you?" Howe asked.

"One of the other guys in charge, Latino dude, he kept shooting people."

Fucking Lopez.

"Captain, I have medical training," said Stewart. "You want me to see to these folks?"

"Absolutely. If Captain Lopez comes by, shoot him in the head."

"Sir?"

"Just do it."

Howe and Shaffer took off, but didn't find much. They decided to go down another flight and double back. It was dark on this floor, but the lights simply seemed out not doing that weird bending thing. Howe gestured to go slower. Soon, they found the bodies. Crushed, mangled, missing pieces, and some in states that defied physics. It was as if they had been rearranged on an atomic level. Glancing both ways, there was a clear path The Imago God had taken from the field. Shaffer tapped his gun and hurried after it.

He didn't make it far.

The artificial god created by the Affiliates reared out of the darkness, all those colors swirling and shimmering in the deeper black amongst the steel, circuitry, and dead flesh. An arm-like appendage came down and bashed Shaffer's head into a pulp as the splatter was drawn into its void. The rest was left to fall.

Howe backed up against the wall. He didn't even raise his gun. It wasn't fear but some other emotion, something he'd never experience before. Hands by his side, eyes wide, there was nothing he could do but take in this unique being.

The Imago God stared back at him with what might have been three white eyes floating in the dark space of what had been shaped as a head for it. No sounds came forth, no great revelations, but Howe understood.

The twelve foot behemoth turned and broke through the final wall.

Within a minute, Lopez and his fire team sprang. They did their best, Lopez cackling the entire time. The Imago God slaughtered all of them, Lopez getting torn apart and his entrails absorbed. Howe had to admit he enjoyed that part.

The sun was rising. He staggered out of The Stadium to watch The Imago God wander off into the jungle. No one else was left to try and stop it. Maybe that was the way it was supposed to be.

Howe sat down on a crate and watched the sun come up. People had started to appear, most likely because the noise had stopped. People were still scared and confused, so he supposed he might have to do something about that. With Lopez dead, the men here from Blockade would back him over Bale if it came to it.

"Hey, you didn't die."

Howe turned to find Vivian standing there in nothing but an oversized hoodie. She was smoking one of her cigarettes, reminding him he still had the ones she gave him. He pulled them out and lit one up.

"You didn't die either. I'm glad."

They smoked quietly for a moment.

"Well, you got something new," said Howe.

Vivian looked at the ground. "Not like this."

"Yeah."

"Did… did you get up close to it?"

"Yeah."

"So you felt it?" asked Vivian.

"I think that's the only reason I'm alive."

Vivian ran a hand through her hair. "How am I supposed to get past that? That I had a hand in making that happen?"

"You didn't know it would be like this."

Vivian flicked her spent cigarette on the ground and went to snuff it out before remembering she was in bare feet. "It didn't want to be here. It lashed out because we created it against its will."

"Aren't we all created against our will?" asked Howe.

Vivian took that in, unsure how to respond.

❧ 4 ❧

ALWAYS FACE DIRECTLY
INTO RUIN

IT WAS ANOTHER PACKED NIGHT. College kids crammed in too tight, chugging back overpriced drinks, talking over music that was cranked up way louder than it needed to be. Connor had complained about the music before. He had a hard enough time hearing orders over the din of voices without someone playing the same track three times in a row. Management didn't care, as long as money was flowing in.

A couple came close to having sex on the pool table, and while he should have said something, he didn't bother. He wasn't paid enough to care. They disappeared into one of the restrooms, and he considered the problem solved. A few of the other bartenders would have rushed over, but for them this job was something important. For Connor, it was only a way to pay his bills while he finished grad school.

The Biology Major was in again. He had tried to talk to her earlier, but the place had been too busy. She was petite, with frizzy blonde hair and huge glasses. Connor had no idea what her name was, but she gave off that nerd vibe that he found himself attracted to. She had never come in with any guys, so he was hoping she was single.

The night came to an end and he was thinking about her

as he went through his shift routines: taking out the trash, wiping down the tables, emptying the overflowing ashtrays that sat outside on the patios. One of his coworkers swept the floor and another counted the stock. The manager counted up the take, and began dolling up the tips.

Connor had done okay, but not as well as he had expected given the crowd. The money here was much better than he would make flipping burgers, but he left most nights with a headache, and the hours were shit. Fortunately, he only had one more year of this to go.

With the bars closing at two, it was tilting past three by the time he got out of the door. Most of the district had settled down by that point, everyone kicked out and ventured home. There were two twenty-four hour restaurants still open, but they looked dead. Connor walked up the street and considered heading over to get something to eat. The leftovers at home didn't sound all that appealing. Considering his budget, he continued on with a sigh.

It was still cold for April. Shoving his hands further into his coat pockets, he hoofed it a little faster to the parking lot. He could've parked the car closer, but it would've cost him ten dollars each time for a pay lot, and he'd decided it wasn't worth it. Of course, at the end of each night, he regretted that choice.

It was standard for him to cut down the alleyway between the guitar shop and the yoga studio. Both were housed in larger buildings, part of the gentrification of the neighborhood. Everybody seemed to have an opinion on how the area was heading except him. Connor wouldn't be around much longer to care. For now, it simply was a way to shave five minutes off his walk.

Turning the corner, he immediately noticed all the security lights were out. Pausing, he considering going around the long way. What a pain in the ass. He just wanted to get home, eat some questionable chili from three days ago, and pass out.

There weren't even any dumpsters down there for anyone to hide behind, the alley not rezoned for them yet. He had been taking this route for months and wondered about it. A conversation with his boss had revealed that little nugget of information. It was literally just an empty space that got littered with trash.

Fuck it.

Connor strode purposely down into the dark, the light at the end quite visible. The alleyway wasn't that long, probably only one hundred and fifty feet. Hell, it was a fifty yard dash. There were no sounds or movements as he drew deeper in, nothing suspicious. It was nothing more than a dark alley filled with garbage. He began to laugh at himself for feeling so scared of it.

Maybe two-thirds of the way through, he heard a giggle behind him.

"Who's there?"

Another little laugh.

Connor fumbled for his phone. Why hadn't he thought about using the flashlight function before? Was he that tired? His fingers shook as he tried to find the buttons; he almost dropped the device. Finally he swiped the right button and the illumination blared to life. Swinging it around, he found a little girl sitting among the trash covered in blood.

"My god, are you okay?"

She didn't look up at him. "You're new, ain't ya, Mister?"

"What?"

"A new member. Welcome!"

"I don't understand," he said, moving closer to her. "Is that *your* blood?"

The little girl lifted a severed human head out of a garbage bag and plopped it onto her lap. She finally looked up at Connor with wild eyes and blood smeared across her mouth. Speckles of it dotted her blonde hair.

"Nope," she replied.

Connor began to back up the way he had come, not even realizing, just recoiling at a base animal instinct level. The child couldn't have been any more than ten, possibly younger. There was a calm ferocity in her face that bespoke a lunacy he had never come across in the flesh.

"So happy to meet'cha, Mister," she said. "We'll play soon."

Connor turned and ran. He bolted back out of the alleyway and onto the main street, mind on fire. At this point, he simply wanted to escape. Nothing else registered. Still clutching his phone with the light on, he sprinted back down to the bar. It didn't occur to him that everything was darker and quieter than before.

Once he arrived, he banged on the door for a good solid minute until he calmed down and realized the obvious: no one was there. Taking a few deep breaths, he turned the flashlight off and thought about what to do next. He could easily call the cops, but standing out here on the streets didn't sound like a great idea. Although he wasn't sure if he could eat now, the diner would have other people. Safety in numbers.

Connor continued back down the street, his destination only another two blocks. Now, however, he began to notice the changes he hadn't when he fled the alleyway. Over half the lights were out now, and those that remained seemed dimmer, more yellowed. It was a sickly glow, giving the revitalized district an ironically decaying atmosphere. Brick crumpled, metal rusted, plants rotted, and wood was ripe with mold. All the colors had been leeched out, as if someone had desaturated an image.

Touching a bench, his fingers came away with flakes attached to them. There was a strong smell of peat and fungus along with something else, a chemical of some sort. Scowling, Connor wiped his fingers off on his jacket.

Behind him there was hollow bang, like someone hitting an empty metal container. Glancing around, he couldn't see where it had come from. There were more noises, but they all sounded far away. They all sounded vaguely industrial, yet there was something odd about them.

He had to get moving.

Near jogging, fears of the diner being abandoned threatened to overwhelm him. With a few more steps, it came into view, bright and full of people. Unable to contain a sob, Connor picked up speed. In his mind, once he arrived, everything would be fine.

About fifty feet from the doors, the lights across the street at the Laundromat began to flicker. Even as he ran, he saw movement in those brief shadows. Something massive, something monstrous. A pointed head to match all those pointed legs.

Connor screamed and burst through the doors.

"Aw, what the fuck is this?"

Looking up from the floor, he found an enormous man with a long black hair and matching beard frowning down at him. He was shirtless, his dark jeans unzipped. Before Connor could get up, the giant reach down and plucked him off the tiles. The giant licked the side of Connor's face and squinted.

"Newbie," he announced to the diner, receiving groans and boos.

Dropped into a booth, he found the diner was very different than how he remembered it. The wood paneling was now darker, splattered with blood and a patina of other stains. The cream tiles were now gray as was the ceiling and partitions, the white tables now black. Even the maroon accents were now a hunter green. It was like some strange mirror-world version of the diner.

Even stranger were the patrons. Half of them were in a state of undress, one man fully nude sitting at the counter. It looked like two people were going at it in a booth in the back. That couple on the pool table seemed so long ago now. Those that were clothed had on an eclectic style of attire, anything from cowboy boots with a suit coat, to three sets of bunny ears color coordinated to match a football jersey.

None of this was as alarming as all the weapons that were assembled and casually strewn about the place.

"What is going on?" said Connor, trying to stop his voice from cracking.

The giant rolled his eyes. Before he could reply, a tall redhead strolled over and sat down across from him. Connor did his best not to acknowledge the fact she was topless.

"Don't mind Garrison," she said. "What's your name?"

"Connor."

"Connor, I'm Lizzie."

"Um, nice to meet you."

"Connor, when did the world change for you?"

"What?"

She sighed. "Tell me what happened."

He told her everything, from leaving the bar to finding the girl and seeing the thing outside the diner to running inside. In telling it, he realized it sounded insane, but neither Lizzie nor Garrison appeared in disbelief. If anything, they seemed more interested in the girl.

"Where was she at exactly?" growled Garrison.

Connor stuttered about the alleyway, the number of blocks up.

Garrison turned to the diner. "Do you hear that? It sounds like we have a straggler from a Butcher Party!"

The diner roared in response, everyone leaping up to get dressed and snag weapons. The flurry of activity shocked Connor, still confused to what exactly was happening. He watched as Lizzie caught a shirt thrown at her and pulled it on over her head.

"Please, what's happening?"

"We call ourselves The Party Crashers. We fuck, then eat, and then we kill The Butcher Party."

"I don't understand!"

People started streaming out the door, screaming in excitement and waving weapons above their heads. Baseball bats, axes, swords, and not a few guns. They looked like a group of people from a lunatic asylum had broke into a costume shop after arming themselves to the teeth.

Lizzie caressed Connor's face. "Once a person steps in here, it's a lifetime membership. This is the world of lies, and you must become a liar to survive. Whatever lies you need to tell yourself, to tell this world. Always face directly into ruin and know there is a beauty in it. Welcome to The Aberrant Lodge."

Then she was gone. They were all gone. The lights were still on, but the diner was empty.

Connor sat there for a while, filled with more questions than answers.

After a while, he got up and looked around. Some food had been prepared but not eaten. It would go bad if they didn't get back soon. He made himself a burger and ate in silence, then cleaned up for some reason. Maybe it some reflex from work, a type of thank you, he didn't know. Finished, he sat back down in the booth, unsure what to do next.

A world of lies. The Aberrant Lodge. None of that meant anything to him.

It had occurred to him they may not be back, or not for some time. Waiting until morning seemed like a good idea, rather than just walking back to his car. Whatever was going on could be tackled then. At this point, dawn wasn't that far off. He checked his phone, but the lock screen was acting weird. The time and date weren't displaying properly. He got it open to the home screen and all his apps seemed fine, yet when he tried to pull one up, it said he didn't have service. So much for calling the cops after all.

One more thing to deal with later. He tried to make himself comfortable in the booth and sleep. Just an hour or two and then he could get to his car in the daylight.

His slumber was fitful and full of nightmares.

Connor awoke with a start and almost fell out of the booth. There was a painful kink in his neck and the smell of the diner had grown pungent. There was no way to tell how long he had been out with his phone still on the fritz, but somehow dawn still hadn't come. That didn't seem possible.

Standing and stretching, he decided to make some coffee. It too had been in-progress, then cleaned away. Supplies gathered back up, half a pot sounded sufficient. While he waited, he wandered back around the diner. His brief attempt at cleaning hadn't stretched to all the sex spills and random food droppings kicked under the tables, which accounted for the stench now. Disgusted, he decided this wasn't his problem. Walking back, he found a stray machete that someone had left shoved behind a table. It came free after three good yanks, his own bargain bin Excalibur.

The coffee had been made strong, but was palatable with cream and sugar. After swallowing back a cup, he started in on a second. Connor kept glancing back between the machete and the windows. It was still dark out, as dark as it had been hours ago. Lizzie's words came back to him and what they implied. The idea that he had fallen into some dark version of his own world sounded like something out of a bad fantasy novel – especially given this world never had sunlight.

It came down to a simple choice – wait or leave.

Connor wasn't a particularly courageous man, but he was easily annoyed. This entire night had irritated him as much as it had terrified him. He just wanted to go home, safe and far away from all this madness. No more bloody children and naked lunatics. Ultimately, that was what prompted him to pick up the machete once more.

Taking the last swigs of the coffee, he headed towards the door. Peering outside, he examined the lights from the Laundromat. They didn't appear to flicker. Out the door and past the diner, Connor took off at a brisk pace. Energized by the nap and the coffee, he decided to loop around and come up onto the parking lot from the parallel street.

All was the same as when he had come down initially. The same grimy, dilapidated version of the city he was used to loomed out in the darkness. Buildings squatted in the gloom, clinging to the shadows as if themselves afraid. The pale light only managed to provide a glimpse of how truly diseased this place was. At least that earthy smell laced with chemicals wasn't as strong here.

Up the side street, past the other bars,everything was thick blackness, periodically interrupted by those yellow lights that failed to illuminate much at all. The noises he had heard before were still audible in the distance, but now Connor was able to discern that odd quality he hadn't been able to put his finger on before. They sounded wet somehow. He shuddered at that implication and kept going.

Another block passed, and he could see perpendicularly down to the hotel. There was activity. People. At first he thought it was The Party Crashers, but just as he began to rush across the street he heard them start chanting.

Moving with far more stealth, he snuck over and peered around the corner of the deli. Connor's mouth dropped in awe.

A wooden X, easily twenty feet tall, had been constructed outside the hotel from assorted timber planks. A creature resembling a harpy from mythology had been impaled on it; her limbs spewed rivers of blood from where the large metal spikes had been driven into her. Her body was stunning, her face more beautiful than any he had ever seen. Even with feathered arms that spread into wings, and her height twice his, she was a marvel seared into his mind. Only her lifeless eyes ruined this image.

About two dozen assembled knelt before the harpy and chanted along with a man who stood on the hotel steps. He wore jeans, a sweater, and bright green top hat like one might wear as a lark for St. Patrick's Day. Holding something out before, he read from it in great fervor.

It took Connor a couple minutes to realize he was reading the ingredients to a bag of BBQ potato chips.

Unsure how to feel, he secreted himself back across the street. Was everyone here insane? He continued towards the parking lot, both confused and appalled. This wasn't a world he wanted any part of.

Finally, the parking lot came into view. Connor sighed, relief washing over him. Part of him knew this might not be completely behind him, but as long as he could make it home, he would happily hide there for a month. As long as he had food and water, he would be fine.

Not far into the lot, one of the two working lights began to flicker. In what felt like slow motion, he turned to see a hand, grossly out of proportion, reach from the strobe effect. Fingers, both long and stubby, protruding out of a fat palm, stretched out on an elastic-like arm free of bones. It came for him. Connor screamed and tried to run.

It swiped at his legs, knocking him to the ground. The machete fell from his grasp, and he swore as he scrambled for it. The hand attempted to wrap itself around his legs with its two longer digits, one of the stubs wiggling up his leg. Connor screamed again as he clawed at one of the digits, pulling it lose, kicking at the other one. For a moment he was free and lunged at the machete. The hand slapped down on him hard, knocking the wind out of him.

Connor choked, struggling to take in air. He blinked, seeing the blade only inches away. As the hand rose up, he threw himself forward and grabbed it. Swinging it up just as the hand came down, he sliced right between its middle and index fingers. In an instant, it retreated back into the flicker.

Laying there panting, Connor stared at the light. It still flickered, but there was no movement. He pulled himself up and waited. Nothing. After another minute, he ran to his car.

At his driver's door, he pulled his keys out and tried to keep it together. No tears, no vomiting, just start the car and drive home.

"Hey, Mister!"

Connor leaned his head again the car.

"I tol'cha we'd play soon."

Connor turned to find the little girl only a few paces away. She was drenched in fresh blood now. There were also dozen or so people behind her, equally soaked in crimson.

"I'm so happy you're here," said the little girl. "We're gonna have a party."

Connor didn't even bother raising his machete. He simply nodded and let the festivities begin.

＃　5　＃

FUTURE EXPRESSIONS

4-14-89

Everything pretty much sucked, but I was used to that.

We were out in what was left of the city, trying to find something that would pass as food. Everyday we strayed a little farther from the treatment plant, a little farther from the illusion of safety. At this point, we knew no help was coming, and our supplies were running short. It had been over a year.

Sierra's voice squawked through my helmet, a series of creative curses. I scurried over the rubble as gracefully as I could in my environmental suit to find her digging away at a refrigerator. Anything she found inside was likely no longer edible, but she seemed determined.

Finally prying the lid back, she peered inside and let out another colorful string of words. Looks like I was right. Good thing we couldn't smell through these suits.

Sierra let the door slam and looked up at me through her visor. "You find anything?"

"A whole lot of fuckall," I replied.

"Where's Snowball?"

I reached down to the comms device on my wrist and tapped the personal security button three times. It was supposed to be used back in the treatment plant in case of an emergency, but we had trained Snowball to come at the sound. That had been a grand experiment resulting in a vast amount of damage, but sure enough, in less than a minute I saw him bounding over the debris towards us.

Sierra climbed up beside me, shaking her head.

"What?" I asked.

"I can't believe we have one of those as a doxxin' pet."

Snowball came to halt in front of us. Its face was humanoid enough, pale gray and almost rock-like. Slightly larger than an average human male's, its expression never hanged. The rest of its body, however, was in a constant state of flux: the size and color of a large polar bear made of a viscous fluid, bending, splashing, and reforming at all times.

We honestly weren't sure what it was. We had discovered it just sitting in the ruins of a house about four months after the world ended. It followed us back to the plant, and at first we were terrified. After a month, I stuck a cat sticker on its forehead and named him Sir Reginald Goopington III. While amused, Sierra argued for Snowball because of the sticker. I allowed her the small victory.

"Do you want to head over towards the gas station?" I asked.

Sierra stared off into the distance. "I'm tired Kendell, Let's just go home."

That worried me. She was always the one who pushed, did the little extra. I likely wouldn't be alive without her. I didn't say anything, however, just nodding and letting her lead the way back. Snowball followed at the rear, flowing and churning along.

Our town hadn't been that big, but it had been hit just as badly as everywhere else when the invasion came. I don't even know if you could call it an *invasion*, per say. It was as if pockets were torn open in the sky all over and nightmares were dumped out onto the planet. I remember watching the feeds, all those black wounds among the clouds, festering and leaking horrors into our world. Yeah, less invaded and more *infected*.

We became overrun with creatures beyond imagination. Some of them you could classify as living beasts, the things from a monster movie, but others were barely describable: lunatic concepts made almost physical. As bad as it was on the ground, it was somehow still worse above. There were reports of aberrations hanging out of those holes, entities that were causing permanent physical and psychological damage to anyone who looked at them. They molded reality like it was a toy; they began to terraform the earth. We now had natural disasters on top of everything else.

Seventeen days. This all only lasted seventeen days.

Then it just ended.

Of course, if you're reading this, you probably know that. Sierra and I survived and I've been keeping a journal about our misadventures ever since. I repeat myself a lot sometimes because I can't remember what I've already written. I'm also very hungry, so my brain is starting to eat itself. Wait no, that's your stomach. Whatever, today was a bust, I'm going to sleep.

4-16-89

I've spent most of the day lying in my makeshift bed reading a book I found. It's not very good, but I have to get my entertainment where I can. With the feeds down, there's not much else. Snowball stood at the foot of my bed, silently. Sierra thinks it's creepy, but I just think of him as a large cat. Honestly.

I have a stack of books I've found over the past month. They're hard to come by these days with almost everything being digital. The newest one I found was thirty years old. At this point, I'm reading to take my mind off the rumble in my belly.

The gas levels were too high to leave the treatment plant today. We have a tiny bit of food stashed away, but only enough to last a couple of days. Sierra is convinced our environmental suits won't be able to withstand it out there. Since she is the engineer, I'm not going to question her on it.

We were damn lucky to be at work when everything went down, all things considered. This toxic waste treatment plant was built to take a nuclear blast. It was meant to incinerate anything, from used medical supplies to outdated paint. A lot of people pictured drums with glowing green ooze coming through here, but it was never anything that cool. Still, there was a lot of stuff you didn't necessarily want to be around, hence the environmental suits.

There had been a lot of upgrades in the last fifty years, especially since the DiCaprio Act of 2041. Workers on the plant floor looked like astronauts now, able to survive extreme conditions. The plant kept us alive those first seventeen days, but it's been the suits keeping us alive when we forage for food since then.

Yeah, Sierra was a chief engineer here. She's kept the lights on in this place, and maintained our suits. I was her best friend before all of this, and she had snagged me a job in the office with their sales department. I was the chick calling other countries telling them to ship their dangerous trash here. Yeah, I know, but I got paid a lot and got to hang out with Sierra.

After rereading the same paragraph three times, I threw the book aside and wandered out of the office. That's where we had bedded down, the spot Sierra had said was the most secure. Inside the plant, we didn't have to wear our suits, so I was usually found in pajama pants and a tank top. The same went for Sierra unless she was working on a project, as she was now. You don't weld in a tank top.

"Hey, you need any help?" I yelled down to her.

Either she was ignoring me or couldn't hear me. Both were equally likely. I was about to come down the steps, when she cut off the welder, and flipped her mask up.

"Oh hey, I just finished. What's up?"

"You need any help?"

Sierra took off her mask and unzipped her jacket. "Nah, I'm good."

In every way that Sierra and I were alike, we were also absolute opposites. We both loved VR games, tequila shots, zar music, tattoos, and men we probably shouldn't get involved with. On the flipside of that, she was a six foot tall blonde Viking with double Ds and a mind for math, while I was barely over five foot, raven-haired, and artistic. A package deal, we had done a lot of dumb shit together over the years.

I sat down on the steps. "You okay?"

She shrugged. "No better or worse than any other day."

"Wanna eat something?"

Sierra glanced down at her project. "I guess."

"Whatcha working on?"

"Air vent needed fixing."

"Cool. I'm glad you're on top of it."

She didn't reply, instead slipping out of her welding gear. Following me back up to the office, we opened the box that held the remainder of our food. A few granola bars, a can of baked beans, a crushed snack bag of chips, and a bottle of vitamins. Fortunately, we had a ton of water, finding a delivery truck in pristine condition about six months ago. Drinking had gone before bathing. So yeah, we stunk.

Sierra popped a vitamin in her mouth and was about to unwrap one of the granola bars when Snowball began freaking out. He skittered around outside the office, and about the plant floor. His form grew wild and erratic, steaks of his body growing a charcoal gray.

We both began swearing as we ran around looking for the rifles.

Sierra found hers first and bolted across the plant floor to the main doors. I had left mine near my bed. Slinging the weapon over my shoulder, I hightailed it over to a ladder on the other side of the office, where broad windows overlooked everything. There, a ladder stretched up to a third level. Climbing as fast as I could, I then crossed a maintenance deck to peer out a set of bay windows.

Being this close to the windows without my suit wasn't all that safe, but there hadn't been time to put it on. We knew what Snowball's reaction meant. Sure enough, I spotted it a mile out.

I froze, all thoughts about the gas or calling to Sierra evaporated. We had seen a handful of remaining creatures after those seventeen days; most we ran from, a few we fought. But nothing, nothing had been like this.

There was a lot of terrified chatter back in those early days. Words like "aliens" and "gods" were thrown around. Sometimes it got specific, with terms like Kullith, The Pantheon of Filth, C'rannah, and Old Ones. At the time, I wasn't sure if I bought into any of that. I had only seen the world end through feeds until they cut out, then walked out of the plant to find a dead planet that was mostly abandoned.

But now I was watching something walk across the earth that was so alien, so unnatural, that I could feel the tears well up in my eyes as the urine ran down my leg.

It was organic, I can say that much. It was made of flesh and what might have been a carapace, like an insect. Maybe I only think that because of the legs. Ten, twelve, I don't know. There was a thick, ropey substance clinging between those legs, some bizarre amalgamation of motor oil and cobwebs. More than matter, there was energy, too. Not fire or lightning, something that moved slower. Duller. I don't know if it made a sound, maybe, but I could feel it. Vibrations? No, there was more of a pattern to it. I swear, looking back, there may have been words.

It veered off out of town and towards the river, disappearing over the hills just as Sierra rushed up behind me. She only caught a glimpse of it before it vanished, but that was enough. Pulling me back towards the ladder, her voice bringing me back to reality.

Cleaned up and changed, I'm back in bed now. I don't know what to think. Part of me doesn't want to go out scavenging tomorrow, even if the gas is cleared up, but I know we need food. I've been the optimistic one, staying positive for the both of us, but how do you face off against something like that?

4-19-89

Okay, today was a good day.

We found a massive stash of food in a rundown house. Hell, we had to snatch a wheelbarrow from next door just to haul it all back. It looks like this dude had managed to scrape it all together then died of natural causes. Heart attack or stroke maybe. He looked in his fifties. We thought about burying him, but there really wasn't time.

Tons of canned goods. Fruit, vegetables, soup, chili, spam, and tuna fish. There were pickles and peanut butter, soda and snack mix, pasta and pop-tarts. To really round out the score, there had big a massive case of stims. We were both single women in our late twenties putting in long hours at our job, so were already stim junkies when the world exploded. Taking a puff on one of those was almost better than the peanut butter.

We both agreed to only take a few days off in celebration. Last time we had kicked back after finding so much food and almost resulted in us starving. We had a modest feast, continued to see if Snowball would actually eat anything, and turned in.

We're okay. We're going to be okay.

4-21-89

I have seen some strange shit in this last year, but today wins the fuckery prize. I'm going to do my best to explain how today went down, and what I saw, but you're going to have to work with me here.

After kicking back for a few days, Sierra began to get restless. Tinkering around the place paid off big time, because it turned out our power cell was nearly depleted. The plant was one of those types of facilities that not only had basic electricity off the grid, but needed a separate source to power the incinerators. Without everything running, the cell should've last decades, but it had gotten damaged somehow in those first seventeen days.

Of course, while I stayed composed, I was screaming inside as she told me this. My mind conjured up the worse scenarios, all of them ending with us being eaten alive in the middle of town. I was very much against being eaten.

However, she explained to me that industrial power cells were a standard size, all approximately four feet long, nine inches in cylindrical diameter, and weighing just over two hundred pounds. Nothing in town would have one, but Sierra was pretty sure she knew were to find some about twenty miles up river. They'd have to take one of the work trucks still parked down in the loading dock.

I can remember gawking at her, already displeased with where this conversation was heading. "You want to head that far out of town on a hunch?"

"I'm pretty confident at least one will still be there. They have a bunch."

"We had one! I can't think of anywhere that could have that many."

Then it hit me. "Oh shit, you wanna go to the nuclear power plant?"

Sierra shrugged. "The place hasn't blown up, so there's probably something worth stealing."

I couldn't argue against her logic, although I did voice my concerns about radiation. She explained to me how nuclear plants worked in 2089, more or less telling me I had nothing to worry about. She estimated we had a month's left of juice, so it was this or take our chances out in town.

Part of me wanted to leave Snowball behind, but he had proven useful in the past. Not only was he great at detecting any creepy things in the vicinity, but on the rare occasion we came across other people, he was the best deterrent imaginable. There were a lot more survivors out there in the first few months after those seventeen days, but not so much any more. The few we came upon now seemed almost feral. I was thinking about that as I loaded the truck up with a few supplies and our rifles. We had snatched those off the bodies of some dead soldiers. They would be useless too if we couldn't charge them off a power cell.

Snowball splashed up behind us, taking all of it in. I was just worried about how we were going to get him into the truck, but he climbed right up and settled into the bed of the truck without us saying a word. Sierra and I exchanged looks. I told Snowball he was a good boy and to keep his head down. Pulling myself up into the cab, I had to wonder once again just how smart our so-called "pet" was.

Doors were closed, locks were engaged, and we were off. Up into the east end of town, we passed the ruins of houses and small businesses. Buildings were smashed and turned into burnt out husks, whole neighborhoods sent sprawling across the landscape. Broken bricks, splintered wood, and shattered glass littered every square foot as far as the eye could see. I could have convinced myself it had been a tornado that had come through here, were it not for the strange yellow fungus that had sprung up on everything this close to the river. It pulsed on the structures still standing, along with some of the materials lying scattered about.

Unfortunately, we were headed farther towards the river.

Leaving the confines of town, we entered an industrial area. We passed a plastics refinery and an old commercial ceramics company. On the other side of the river sat the massive hydraulic fracturing plant, long out of use. There were similar sites along this stretch, half of them closed years before the planet checked out.

This whole time, Sierra had been gunning the engine and speeding us along. She handled the truck well at nearly seventy MPH, while I rode literal shotgun, my rifle at the ready. We didn't see or hear a thing. Unfortunately, we had to go through another town before we came to the power plant complex, a pleasant little speck that might have surprises. Sierra slowed down to fifty as battered houses loomed at on us from both sides.

It looked to be as badly hit as our neighborhood was. One whole section of the hillside had been gutted with some type of explosion, taking out dozens of houses. On the other side of the street, I could see that foul, sickly yellow trailing up the side of a few wrecked buildings. In my mind, it didn't smell like normal fungus. Instead of dirt, all I could think of was pus. Breathing, living pus.

I choked back the bile rising in my throat and gripped my gun tighter.

We made it through the small town without incident, and I noticed Sierra's scowl. "What?"

"I dunno, that was easy."

"You wanted it hard?" I asked. "I'm sorry, would you like to go back and find some cannibals to get into a firefight with? We can do this! Gloss some cannibals in the face!"

Sierra snorted. "Bitch, shut up."

The truck rolled down hill, the power plant in sight. The four stacks jutted high into the air, cold and still. The whole operation had ceased functioning. The way Sierra had explained it, had something like this happened in the past, it might have been catastrophic, but new measures had been implemented to prevent meltdown. Now they were just some big towers with a bunch of sweet, sweet power cells waiting for us to steal.

Sierra slammed the brakes only a feet away from a short metal bridge. About a hundred feet long, it didn't look in the best of shape. It had definitely taken some hits: one of the guardrails was gone, the other leaning at a slight angle. There was no way to tell how sturdy it was.

Sierra climbed out of the truck and inspected it closer. The bridge went over a small access road cut into the earth beneath. The drop wasn't far, but it was enough. Taking a few tentative steps out onto the metal, it didn't shake or bow. Looking back at me, I threw up my hands.

"Fuck it," said Sierra, heading back to the truck.

As soon as she started gunning it over the bridge, I knew this had been a mistake. The metal began to sway and buckle. I heard her swearing profusely as she punched the gas. Closing my eyes, I recall thinking this might go in my top five dumbest ways to die.

But we got across, the bridge still standing, too. An obligatory high five was in order, and then I checked on Snowball out the back window. He peered up at me with that zero-emotion face. Parts of him rippled, and I hoped he was just having fun going for a ride.

All the gates were wide open and there wasn't a soul in sight. Sierra was positive she knew where to go and steered the truck towards one of the larger buildings: a squat, cement block. The doors were locked, but we just smashed in a window. Once inside, with the lights on from our helmets,

Sierra had a couple wrong turns before going down a short hallway. Shouldering open a heavy metal door, her eyes lit up like it was Christmas.

There was a bank of power cells, twelve in all.

She marveled at the sight. "If I'm right, there will be three other buildings like this."

"So, how many do we take?"

Sierra quickly did some calculations in her head. "If all the cells are still there, we could take six from each unit. Half. This place will still be able to run."

"One cell would already last us forever," I said. "We don't need, uh, many."

"No, but we are taking three from here. Just in case."

Sierra knew how to power down and extract each cell from its unit safely, none of them damaged. We took three that were barely depleted. The cells were heavy as hell, but fortunately some lovely individual had left a dolly in the room. Lugging three of them out still wasn't fun. Snowball shifted out of the way and let us place each one in the back of the truck with him. I'd like to add: he didn't help.

Getting back in the truck, Sierra tapped her fingers on the steering wheel. "I'm not looking forward to trying that bridge again."

"Same. There's always the back way."

She eyed the sky through her visor. "On a normal day, that's an extra thirty minutes. We have no idea what it's like across the river."

"We have food, we have cells. We can either risk it on the bridge, a danger we know, or the back way, which is unknown."

Sierra grimaced. "Stop making sense."

"Plus we have Snowball," I added. "He'll let us know if things get icy."

"I'm already done with this frigid shit," she said, putting the truck into gear.

The nuclear power plant complex was a few miles across, and we didn't run into any trouble. The bridge on the other side was far larger than the one we had crossed, this one going over the river; it appeared to be in perfect shape. We made it over without incident and started back.

I hadn't been this way in years, and wasn't all that familiar with it. I kept scanning the surroundings looking for anything out of the ordinary, but it was hard for me to tell. It all looked the same as it had everywhere else.

We were navigating around a tree that had collapsed out into the road when I spied something down closer to the river. At first it simply looked like any other structure, one miraculously not blown to pieces. There were a number of houses along the bend here, some still retaining three whole walls and others a pile of wreckage. This stood out, rising easily five stories high, far above the rubble.

I motioned for Sierra to slow down, and pointed to it. She immediately pulled off, stopped the truck, and pulled out the set of imaging goggles we had. Flipping them through thermal, to night vision, to distance, she swore as she examined the site.

"What?" I asked.

"Take a look."

She handed me the goggles and I gazed down through the open window. They were maybe a mile away, easily close to a hundred. Humans. Or they had been. That yellow fungus clung to them, and had transformed them. Portions of their flesh had been devoured to allow throbbing growths to form, tumor-like masses. Limping, hunchback, deformed, drooling, most of them were dedicated to the construction of this building using supplies from the area. I couldn't help but think the building looked like a child's crayon scribble of a church.

The whole process looked incredibly crude. Half the time, it seemed like they were using rocks as hammers, kitchen utensils as nails. I think one of them sawed off part of his hand while working, and bled a path across the littered grass carrying a hunk of wood until he fell over. I could tell they were muttering something, but I couldn't make it out.

I turned to hand Sierra the goggles back when Snowball lost it.

Before she even had a chance to floor it, five of the fungus people had swarmed our trunk. They looked even worse up close. It had worked its way into their faces, their eyes dried up and raisin-like while their teeth had become soft and waxy. Their clothing in rags, it had fused to their body with little dots of yellow all over them. The growths were bulbous and thick, layers upon layers of new, alien flesh.

"Un... unbelievers!" one of them managed to gush through the thick spittle in their mouth.

A mucus-rich chorus rang out. "Unbelievers!"

I fumbled for my rifle, trying to aim it out the window.

Turns out, that was unnecessary.

Snowball erupted from the back of the truck and flew into action. In a whirlwind motion, his semi-liquid body also took on a solid state, what I can only describe as blades morphing out of his form. He furiously spun around the truck, dismembering the attackers in moments, and I mean like in *pieces*. The whole event took thirty seconds, max.

Then, the danger over, Snowball stopped in front of my window, his stoic face leaning in. What do you say to that?

"You are such a good boy, Snowball. My good big boy! Please get back in the truck, okay?"

And he did.

We returned to our plant without incident, new cell installed. Sierra is sleeping and I'm writing this. I'm writing this because I'm trying to keep my shit together.

I have no idea if mushroom people are building a church or why, but I'm not thrilled about it. Snowball has never actively attempted to protect us before, so that's new. He's been an alarm system, sure, but we've fought off humans and monsters alike while he's just stood there in the past.

Not sure which situation is going to keep me up tonight.

4-22-89

I tried playing with Snowball today, actually tried gauging his intelligence. It didn't go so well. He follows us around like a dog, and understands some basic commands, but only when he wants to. Sierra is convinced the cat sticker is appropriate. At the time, I just thought it was funny.

I've tried to get him to pick out colors and shapes, but he's shown no ability for that, or at least, no interest. I got him to fetch twice, then I think he got bored. Honestly, I got the distinct impression he thought I was an idiot and kept dropping the ball. You can pick up slight distinctions in the way he moves. We know for a fact that black only appears within his form when creatures are near, but I've noticed other subtleties. His waves cascade more gently when he's happy or calm, whereas he takes on a more blotchy aspect when he's agitated. Makes sense.

We opened some of the canned goods that night, and I tried to push a peach into his mouth. It was stuck there for two hour before I pried it back out. That rocky façade never changed, never showed emotion. It was like whoever made him only had a rough understanding of what a face was supposed to be for and slapped one on him because they thought it would screw with humans.

We rarely played music out loud in the plant, because even with its walls, we were worried someone would hear. Sierra was fixing one of the lights however, and I had charged a deck player. I put on a playlist, not thinking much about it as I handed tools up to her. Zar beats softly came out and suddenly Snowball was next to us.

"Woah, what's up with him?" Sierra asked.

Intrigued, I turned up the music, letting it flood the plant.

Snowball began to dance. His body shifted and shaped itself in time with the music, dipping and shimmied around the floor. It was like watching a vid off the feed; he thumped in sync with every beat, flowed with every e-string. Sierra had climbed down, wide-eyed. When the song ended, she hit pause, but we both clapped.

"That was a little loud," I said. "But damn."

Snowball stood there as if nothing had happened.

4-28-89

So yeah, we've been dealing with some stuff.

A few days ago, we were out looking for supplies when we saw some of the fungus people in the distance. Here, in our town. Ten or twelve of them, fumbling around through the market district. That's part of downtown, not far from the river. We hid, but kept our guns at the ready. They must not have been close enough to set off Snowball, because he hung back, too. Eventually they disappeared, but this was not a good sign.

The next day, we headed up the hill to get a better layout of the area. There was a great spot in what had used to a mechanic's shop to look out over the town and see well across the river. We had used this vantage point a few times the past year to scope out sites we hadn't plundered supplies from yet. But this time it was different. We spied a handful of fungus folk doing who-knows-what on our side, with a hell of a lot more on the other side.

The town on the opposing side of the river had been hit far worse than us. Most of the hillside had collapsed onto it, burying what remained of the buildings. We all lived in a valley, but it was as if an entire section of a topographical map had been rearranged over there. I don't know how our side wasn't more impacted.

I assume the fungus people were looking for us, but Sierra didn't think so. They appeared to be building things. From this distance, it was impossible to make out, even with the goggles. Neither of us had any desire to inspect any closer.

"Knowing those freaks, it's probably another church," I said.

"I dunno," replied Sierra. "Multiple projects, smaller works."

I sat back against the wall, dust billowing up around my suit. The number one priority for most living things now was survival. Glancing around the hollowed out building, there weren't even signs of animals besides a few obligatory cockroaches. Not nests, no scat, nothing. Just charred wood, broken glass, and few leftover pieces of machinery.

"What could they want?" I asked. "What could be driving them?"

"Those mushroom fuckers, who knows? A pizza?"

We laughed, but we found out the next day.

I had named them "Spooky Deer." They were like your average deer, but completely skinned, with black antlers, and with long-fingered human hands. They were horrifying. That said, by the time we had reached the top of the hill again, the fungus gang had already engaged in a battle with them and nearly wiped them out. Only a few were left out of the dozens that had been on the hillside, those now dispatched with the weapons built from the previous day. We couldn't make out was they were shrieking to the sky, but it was bellowed with each kill.

"They were preparing for war," said Sierra.

"No," I said. "Genocide. Remember what they said at the truck? 'Unbeliever'. They're going to spread out and kill everything that's not them."

Back at the plant, I lay in bed and wondered about all of it.

A cult of fungus people, deer monsters, giant bug creatures. I had seen what looked like babies with bat wings flying in formation outside the windows one night and what I swore was a jellyfish smashing in a soda machine. Some of my recollections were hazy to say the least. Had there really been a naked, golden woman floating over the river back during those seventeen days? Had I really heard voices arguing high above, or just in my head? No one really knew what exactly had happened here on earth.

The next day we didn't have to go far. From a discreet hiding spot, we watched as the fungus people began to pour across the bridge onto our side of the river.

Sierra shifted her gun. "We might have to find a new place to crash."

I am not pleased.

4-24-89

Alright, this is heavy…

We decided not to take the truck scouting because it would make too much noise. If we found a backup location, we could always make a run for it with all our supplies loaded up then. We hoped we didn't have to abandon the plant, but we knew it might be a possibility.

All the places in town worth hunkering down in we had already looted. Police station, hospital, fire station, even the library. The high school was on the edge of town, at the top of the hill, and the water treatment facility was much farther down river. We didn't know which direction the horde would go, and worried about making the wrong decision. After mulling it over, we decided to head for the school since the fungus people seemed more inclined to stay by the river.

It was a good two mile incline hike. We were both in far better shape than we had been before all of this, but poor nutrition was a factor. We got winded quickly even with the stims, and had to take frequent breaks.

The trek up was more of the same. Whole swatches of neighborhoods eradicated, vehicles hurled through town like toys, impaled on utility poles, massive crater-like footprints where some unknowable behemoth had walked for a short time before vanishing.

Not a single corpse lay among the ruins.

I never questioned it, never allowed myself to think about it. I didn't want to know. Sometimes the lack of bodies added to the isolation, the loneliness that weighed heavy on both of us. We had each other, but it got so quiet. No car horns, no birdsong, no children laughing. The world slowly got emptier and emptier.

Finally we made it up to the plateau where the high school sat. One side of it had been crushed, but the other wing appeared pristine. There would be multiple entrances to try, but Sierra was most interested in the gym. She was convinced they would have a unit in there for a cell since it was built as a crisis shelter.

We were about to sneak around the corner when were heard a commotion in the parking lot. Before we could check in out, something that had once been human leapt out in front of us. Naked and covered in blood, his face was a jumbled mess that almost resembled fangs and a snout. He took us in with ravenous intent.

"Death to the yellow disciples!" he roared. "All hail Manaha!"

Sierra blasted him in the chest with her rifle.

Fucking cannibals.

It would seem those lunatics had grown more organized. They had been fighting it out with the fungus people, both sides taking heavy losses. It had been all melee weapons so far, so we rushed in and started tagging off any leftover survivors. All riled up, Snowball joined in. I was terrified, never in a battle for my life before, but we had the advantage despite their numbers.

It ended with me shaking, and the rest of them dead except one cannibal bleeding out.

Sierra stormed over to him, foot on his chest, gun aimed at his head. "Why were you fighting them?"

"The gods, the gods sought a new battleground," he said, choking on the words. "But we were left to claim victory… our chosen, we… our messiah will see to it your feeble god will fall."

"But you're human," I said.

The cannibal sputtered up blood. "Was! Now more, now a godling! I serve as you serve."

"What?"

His eyes went to Snowball and then over to the gym. "Isn't… that why you're here?"

"Ah, for fuck's sake," said Sierra before putting two shots into his head.

We looked at each other, then at the gym.

I could tell Snowball was acting weird. Looking back, I realize he was getting paler, accumulating white streaks. We tried the doors but they were locked. Losing patience with the whole day, Sierra blasted the doors open and we strolled in. Taking a left, we strolled into the gym.

Both of us stopped, stunned.

That's when Snowball, behind us, opened his mouth and started singing.

———

4-27-89

It's been a few days again, and I'll try to catch everything up.

The fungus people aren't a threat anymore as far as I can tell. Pretty sure they're all dead. Not sure what would've happened if anyone got in the gym before us, but it's not an issue now.

Six hundred and twelve entities just like Snowball, hanging out on the gym. From what I can gather, they were waiting there for someone to come along and, I don't know, turn them on? Whatever Snowball said to them did the trick, because now all of them are as dedicated to us as he is.

I came up with a theory based on what the cannibal told us. What if earth was just a field for all these gods to play on, one of many? Once the big game is over, they leave their fans to bicker and fight until somebody claims dominance. It sounds dumb, but it makes sense in a way. But get this, what if one of these assholes thought it would be funny to leave a bunch of weapons in the hands of the humans, give them a fighting chance? The faces aren't to screw with us, it's to let us know these are ours.

Currently Banana and Bulldozer are helping Sierra move steel girders to reinforce a door. Gold Star, Pumpkin, Old Glory, and Hotdog are on sentry, while Santa Claus and Rainbow watch from the roof. Thumbs Up, Crossbones, and Rose are clearing the bay door area of debris. That's just off the top of my head. Snowball, of course is next to me, as I type this.

The current issue I'm having with the apocalypse? It's hard to find stickers.

YOUR ACOLYTE EYES

I HATE when people say that truth is subjective. Your perception of events may be up for debate, but facts are facts. Problem is, I don't know the truth, and I'll be the first to say my perception is highly questionable.

Let me start at the beginning.

It had taken months to hammer out plans for the camping trip. Everyone was so busy anymore, lives filled with responsibilities and distractions. Events like this had been easier to pull off back in our twenties, but we all had big kid jobs now. Hell, my brother Neal and Katie had an actual kid.

There had been some argument over how this trip was going to go down. Neal and David wanted to rough it, while Katie and my wife, Lucy, leaned towards an upscale cabin with a hot tube. I didn't care. David's wife Bethany was just happy to have a few days off from work. After some searching, we found a middle ground at the edge of Ohio in a private park that seemed to make everyone happy.

Lucy and I rode down with Neal and Katie, while David and Bethany followed in his truck. It was loaded with all our gear, enough supplies to last us a week, let alone a weekend. The wives had a grand time talking about my nephew, singing to music, and generally enjoying the drive. We didn't get to see my brother and sister-in-law as much as I would've liked. Ten years ago, back in college, we had all been drinking together almost nightly.

It took us little less than two hours to reach McKinley, Ohio. I wouldn't say it was even a fully realized town, just a smattering of rundown houses, a general store advertising a number of generic items, and a gas station that looked like it hadn't been open in decades. Everything was crumbling and grayed. The few people on the street gawked at us as we drove past, one woman open-mouthed and bug-eyed. Her gaze followed our car as it disappeared down the block. It was unnerving, but I chalked it up to small town mentality.

The GPS turned us right up the hill. McKinley Park. There wasn't much here. A large pond that had been touted online as a fishing lake, a rusted out playground, two stone pavilions with shingled roofs that looked in disrepair, and a few other buildings in the distance. Beside the parking lot was a residential house, a man mowing the lawn out front. We parked as he shut off the machine.

Neal climbed out with a wave. "Hey there, we're here about the Adirondack cabin site."

"Ayup."

"Do we need to sign in or anything?"

The caretaker was easily six and half feet tall, stick thin, with an unkept beard and long hair. Brilliant blue eyes never wavered from Neal. I took a step forward, but he reached into his pocket and pulled out a pack of cigarettes and lit one up.

"Keep down the road, first turn on your left. The campsite is up the hill. Truck'll make it no problem, but the car won't get up there. You'll have to leave it in the lot."

Before we could say anything, he returned to his mowing.

We all looked at each other. There had been no mention about possible inaccessibility on the website. Katie was already bitching, but David offered to drive up and scope out the scene. Bethany rode with him, while we waited.

Katie folded her arms. "This is a shit show."

"Nah," said Neal. "This is great!"

Lucy went over to commiserate with Katie as Neal wandered off to look around. While I figured my wife would put that clinical therapist training to use, I lit up one of my own cigarettes and worried about the weekend. If it had been just me, I wouldn't have cared. Nihilism is a fine philosophy when you're a solo act.

I tried to tell myself that there was nothing wrong with the park. Obviously, the caretaker was attempting to keep up with it. They probably had very limited funds. Using whatever hype they could on the website brought in desperately needed tourists. It was all easily explainable.

And yet...

The gravel looked sharper than it should, like each piece had been filed to achieve the maximum amount of edges. The grass looked sickly, as if the earth was poisonous. Were those bloodstains on the swing set, there in a patina among the rust? I swore I could smell the pond from here, something foul and rotting, something creating a thick film on the top of the water. There in the trees, movement, sinister and hidden.

"Ben?"

I spun to see Lucy examining me, frowning.

"Are you okay?" I asked her.

"Are *you* okay?" she replied. "I just watched you chain smoke three cigarettes in row, and you're kind of twitching."

"Looking. Watching."

She sighed. "Did you take your meds this morning?"

Shit. I hadn't. Everything had been so hectic. And they were in the truck. I told her as much, and she hugged me. David would be back soon.

Just as she said that, he rolled back down the hill.

Lucy put her arm around me. "See, they're back. Everything is fine. No worries, baby."

Standing there, watching the truck come towards us, I felt like an idiot. I had done it yet once again. About ten years ago, I was diagnosed with severe bipolar disorder type I with ultra-rapid swings, and about four years ago given a second diagnosis of obsessive compulsive personality disorder. Either of those alone would be hard enough to manage, but together, they could fuel paranoia and delusions. I took a cocktail of mood stabilizers and antipsychotics, four pills twice a day. If I missed them even once, things could get weird. Fortunately Lucy knew me well enough to notice when I started getting askew.

I noticed all the gear had been unloaded from the back of the truck. I gestured towards the empty bed. "I'm taking that as a good sign?"

"Oh yeah, climb in," said David.

Katie glanced around. "Where's Neal?"

David pointed. He was jogging back from one of the buildings. I hadn't noticed the mower stop, and the caretaker had disappeared. I tried to push thoughts of that from my head. It didn't matter.

Neal made his way up to us, grinning. "There's a pool over there!"

"Really?" asked Katie.

"No water in it, of course."

"You're an ass."

We climbed into the back of the truck and David kicked it into gear. Down the road and turned at the first left. Up the hill, we were barely on a path. Here in late May, the woods were green and lush, flowers everywhere. The trees rose up above us, creating a canopy. Afternoon sunlight broke through in shafts, causing everyone to marvel at the beauty. The truck took a few more turns then rose higher. The trees here were bigger, older. This was Appalachian Country, the piedmont. Depending on how big this property was, there could have easily been sections never before touched by humans.

The hill started to bend, and there stood a small building. Constructed out of tan brick, it was maybe six feet by six feet, and almost eight feet tall. A wooden door was affixed to its front had a crescent moon cut out near the top.

"What the hell is that?" asked Lucy.

I laughed. "I'm guessing that's the outhouse."

Katie immediately began screeching, but I wasn't paying attention. We had turned a bend and arrived. It was far better than I had expected.

The clearing was the size of a small parking lot, I'd say roughly fifty feet by maybe ninety feet, but hardly an exact rectangle. There were two large trees in the clearing along with a rickety picnic table, a large pile of firewood, and a massive fire pit in the center about six feet in diameter. It looked to be made of the same brick that the outhouse had been constructed from. Along the perimeter, nestled among the treeline, were six Adirondack cabins. Built out of wood on top of poured concrete slabs, they had fourteen foot long backs, seven foot sides, angled roofs, and open fronts. All of the gear sat in a pile off by one of the cabins.

The clearing was free of debris and garbage, the cabins in great condition. Even the picnic table would be fine with a tablecloth. The place was beautiful, the summer sun streaming down and the air full with the scent of wild flowers. My mood had done a one-eighty, captivated with the sight. Everyone else felt the same.

"This is stunning," said Lucy.

"I going to play with all the animals," announced Bethany. "And they will all be my friends."

David snorted. "Despite what you want to believe, you're not a cartoon princess."

She gave him two middle fingers and danced around the truck.

It took a few hours to get everything set up. We'd brought quite a bit of stuff. Two fold out tables, two canopies, six chairs, sleeping bags, pillows, backpacks, cooking supplies, grill for the fire, booze, bottled water, coffee, USB charger, blutooth stereo, and extra tents just in case. Yeah, we were "glamping." But everyone was happy, and that's what counted.

It was around six when we had finally finished and David offered to start dinner. Mechanical Engineer may have been his day job, but cooking was his passion. Just to be pretentious, he told us he was making gourmet grilled cheese – melted gouda and provolone with crumbled real bacon and a spicy aioli sauce on brioche bread. The pasta salad was already made and chilled. He wouldn't tell us what was in store for tomorrow.

David ran around playing chef while the rest of us hit the booze. Neal and Katie looked through the selection, in typical beer snob fashion, while Lucy and Bethany talked shop. Bethany had just been promoted to associate director at the assisted living facility she worked at, and seemed to enjoy that role better than being a floor nurse. Lucy had been offered a management position in a state psychiatric facility, but wasn't sure if she wanted to leave private practice. It was all way above my pay grade.

Neal walked up and handed me a hard cider. "How you doing, man?"

"I'm good. Better. I forgot my pills this morning, so I was a little shaky there for a bit."

"Yeah, I could tell. Figured I'd give you some space, check in when it seemed right."

Neal always knew how to handle me, I'll give him that. A lot better than our parents. Our mom honestly believed screaming was the best course of action in any situation.

We shot the shit as he played with the fire. Katie was trying to find a different job, and their son Adam was in daycare. He asked about my next book, but I brushed it off and mentioned the latest designing gig I had pulled off. My brother either didn't notice or didn't say anything. I didn't want to talk about my stalled writing career.

Dinner was served and it was spectacular. Somehow David had juggled it so most of the sandwiches were all done right around the same time. Cheesy, yummy goodness. They paired great with the bite from the dressing on the pasta salad. I cracked open another cider and smiled at Lucy.

Bethany said she was going to brave the outhouse and we all yelled various ill omens at her as she strolled away. Spiders, bears, ghosts, serial killers, cannibal hillbillies. Whatever we could think of. It was right down the incline, you could see it from the top cabin, so no one was actually worried. It was still bright out, and we were all laughing.

I don't know how much time passed. Long enough for me to finish my cider and open another one. We were all sitting around the fire pit, joking and carrying on.

Katie stood up. "Um, I need to pee."

"Thank you for announcing that," I said.

"Bethany still isn't back yet."

Our heads all turned in the direction she had left.

David shrugged. "Bang on the door and tell her to hurry up."

David was joking but I could tell the vibe had shifted.

Katie turned to her husband. "You're coming with me."

With a sigh he got out of his chair. They left the fire pit and made their way out of the clearing. Lucy opened her mouth to say something, then closed it. I wondered what she was going to say. David didn't seem all that concerned. Was Bethany playing some prank on everyone? I could see her doing that. I could also see David acting like he didn't care. He veered into that toxic masculinity bullshit sometimes.

Then Katie screamed and David was running faster than I could even get out of my chair.

Lucy and I weren't too far behind him when he reached the outhouse. Katie had backed away, hand over her mouth. Neal was holding the door open, looking more confused than anything else. We raced around the corner and David was in the outhouse before any of us could stop him.

"Bethany? Bethany! Baby, are you okay?"

But she wasn't okay. She was… I don't know. Her shorts around her knees, toilet paper still clutched in her hand, it looked like she was frozen in mid scream. Her already large blue eyes were stretched open, tears running down, her mouth gaping.

David pulled her off, screaming for help. Lucy rushed in and yanked up her underwear and shorts. Getting her outside, her body started to relax from its previous rigid state. She was obviously still alive, but something had happened.

"I have, like, basic first aid training guys," said Lucy. "She's alive but her pulse is racing. I have no idea what's going on her. Seizure, stroke, maybe bitten by something?"

David started to pick her up. "We need to carry her back to the truck."

Neal, David, and I lifted Bethany as carefully as we could and hauled her back to the campsite. Each step we took, she grew more and more, loose in our arms. Finally she started looking around. As we neared the truck, she crossed her legs and wrapped her arm around David's neck.

"Babe, just out of curiosity, what the fuck are you guys doing?"

David motioned for us to lower her. "Jesus, are you feeling okay?"

"Uh, yeah. Why wouldn't I be?"

We filled her in on everything that had just happened, how we had found her and what she had looked like. Bethany stole one of my cigarettes to smoke while she pondered these revelations over. She said she was super tired, that was all. Mostly she was amused that everyone got to see her half naked.

"We're getting you to a hospital," said David.

Bethany shook her head. "Forget it, I'm not ruining the weekend. I'm pretty sure I had some kind of seizure, a petite mal or a tonic. Of course it's the fucking nurse who gets some weird ass medical issue in the middle of the woods."

Lucy looked dubious. "Do you have any history of seizures or epilepsy?"

"Not that I know of, but it could be a lot of things. Listen, I know my body and I know my training. I'll be okay for now. Let me take a nap. I promise, if anything happens again, I'll head straight to the nearest urgent care."

None of us were pleased, but what could we say? We couldn't *make* someone who had possession of their wits go to hospital. We didn't know any better, and if she said there wasn't anything to worry about, all we could do was shrug. David got her settled in one of the cabins and came back to the fire pit. The next few hours were spent quietly drinking and having conversation, all of us trying to ignore the tension that had grown in the clearing. As dusk fell, David crept over to check on his wife. I didn't realize I had been holding my breath until he returned smiling. She was snoring.

"So she's okay?" asked Katie.

David shrugged. "I guess. She may be a spazz when it comes to everyday life stuff, but she's a damn good nurse. If she says she'll be fine, I'm going to believe her."

I still didn't like it, but who was I to say anything?

One of the bottles of tequila was broken into and passed around. Stories were shared, many of them exaggerated. The night grew darker, shadows giving way into the full black. No one had wanted to walk back down to the outhouse, even the girls electing to squat behind a tree, but now I needed to do more than just pee. Lucy offered to walk with me, but I told her it was fine. Grabbing a flashlight from the cabin we had claimed, I began the trek down the path.

You could barely see the stars through the tree branches above. The glow of the fire had already been swallowed up by the darkness behind me as I went down the slight decline. Up ahead, the outhouse sat silent. I opened the door, ready to see Bethany's face pulled back in horror again, but there was nothing. Slipping inside, I hurried up and attended to business. The flashlight sat on the floor, shinning up at the ceiling, while every tiny sound echoed in the small brick room. Finished, I stepped out and swung the light out into the trees. Nothing. But it didn't feel like that.

I returned to camp and said nothing. Instead, I downed a few more gulps of tequila and smoked too many cigarettes. About two hours later, Neal and Katie said they were crashing out and David agreed, stating he wanted to make sure he was up with Bethany in the morning. Lucy helped me stagger to bed and I was out within minutes.

I'm not sure when I woke up. It was still dark, the fire burning down. I was also still drunk. I rolled over and Lucy was gone. Struggling to pull myself up, I looked out into camp and saw her with Bethany. I think, at the time, I wasn't sure what I was seeing. It appeared that both of them were naked, Lucy kneeling in the grass while Bethany danced around her sprinkling her with glowing embers. That didn't seem right, though. At the time I didn't care, Lucy was right there and she was fine, so I collapsed back into my pillow.

The next morning was rough. I couldn't drink in my thirties the way I had in my twenties. Fifty year old alcoholics do it because they do it every day, but I was a casual drinker now and my body wasn't adapted to it anymore. Everything hurt, plus I had forgotten my meds again last night. I swallowed them down with a swig of water and stumbled my way to the fire pit. I was the last one up.

"Morning, precious," said Neal, with a grin. "You look like shit."

"You wish you looked this good."

David poured a cup of coffee from a camp pitcher. "Does baby want his bottle?"

"Gimme!"

Bethany was feeling great and ready to hit the day running. Her and Lucy were giggling about something, and the foggy memory of them from the previous night teased at the back of my mind. I'd ask about it later, but I was far too concerned about the coffee that was saving my life at the moment. Everyone was in a good mood, except Katie, who was tearing through their cabin.

"Hey Neal, have you seen my phone?"

"Weren't you on it at dinner last night?"

She shook her head. "I was using yours to show Lucy pics of Adam. I haven't had mine since we… damn it."

"What?"

She flopped down in the chair beside him. "We were using it to play music in the car."

I shrugged. "Okay, you found it."

She gave Neal a look. "Adam."

"Fuck," said Neal. "Her parents are watching Adam. If something's wrong, they'll call her phone. Sure, they can call mine, but we don't want to worry them."

"I'll drive you down," said David.

"Nah, I'll just walk," said Neal. "It's not far."

Neal kissed Katie, grabbed the keys and headed out. It was around ten in the morning. David popped open a cooler and produced a carton of eggs, a package of ground sausage, and a bag of frozen home fries. All of it eventually got cooked together in a cast iron skillet over the fire, seasoned, and topped with shredded cheese. People who thought camp food was hotdogs and trail mix had never met David.

Time passed, and eventually I decided to break into the

beer. A nice hefeweizen today. I figured I'd get a glare from Lucy, but she was too involved with Bethany. I think they were talking about music, something about "acolyte eyes." Katie was anxious, so I got her going on about my nephew. At some point David joined in, and we lost track of time.

Finally David pointed out that Neal had been gone for almost two hours. Katie hadn't wanted to say anything and be *that* wife, but she was getting worried. Bethany shushed her, assuring her that any concerns were valid. We discussed what do to next, and of course that turned into a small argument. Everyone had a different idea how best to proceed. Finally, it was decided that Katie, Lucy, and I would follow the path back down to the parking lot while David and Bethany would wait here with the truck, in case Neal returned.

It was shortly after noon when we headed out. The path wasn't hard to follow, a truck had managed it and we had just drove up it yesterday. It took only forty minutes or so to make it to the road, another five to reach the car. There it was, just sitting there where we left it. No Neal, and Katie could see her phone inside.

"Well, at least we know he never made it to the car," I said.

Katie spun on me. "That's a good thing?"

"That's one piece of information we didn't have before."

We made our way back up, calling out for Neal. I was now officially on edge. I couldn't see how my brother had gotten lost. Had he gotten hurt somehow? Attacked or abducted? Had whatever afflicted Bethany stricken him, his rigid body laying in the tall grass only yards away from us?

Again I found the woods threatening. Once beautiful and idyllic, it now matched the rest of the park. It was a mask, used to lure in the unsuspecting until it was ready to reveal the malevolence that festered beneath. As my voice grew more desperate, the more I believed in what I was thinking. There was a presence here, inhospitable and perverse.

Our voices rang out, but Neal never answered.

We passed the outhouse and came to the top of the incline, the three of us stopping in shock. The truck was gone. Racing down, we called out for David and Bethany, trying to figure out what could have happened. All of our gear was still there, the fire still going. Katie started screaming when there was a rustling in the nearby cabin.

Bethany popped her head out. "Hey guys, did you find… where the fuck is the truck?"

According to Bethany, shortly after we had left, she hadn't been feeling good and laid down. David had been playing on his phone when she had gone to the cabin, the truck where it had been the whole time. Lucy wondered if he had somehow driven past us, but I couldn't see how that was possible. I told the girls to stay put and walk down to the outhouse.

The road up the hill came to a bend at the outhouse, turning left up the incline to the campsite. There was a path there, but it was barely big enough to get a four wheeler on. I stood there, examining the path, looking for any sign that a massive 4x4 truck would've passed through. I really didn't know what clues I hoped to find, but I didn't see anything that jumped out at me.

Stepping back towards the outhouse, I paused. I don't know why, but I knew I should look inside. I didn't want to. Swearing to myself, I flung the door open expecting to find David in the same state we had found Bethany.

Nope. Worse.

There was nothing but blood.

Blood everywhere, spilled on the floor, some splattered on the walls, and even a tiny bit dripping from the ceiling. Nothing else but blood. A pint, a gallon, it was hard to gauge. Enough to make an impact.

I slammed the door and fell back into the dirt. I wanted to believe an animal had been killed in there, *needed* to believe that. But I didn't.

I went back to camp. Katie was crying, and although I expected Lucy to be consoling her, my wife didn't seem terribly concerned. I told them about the path, and told them an animal had died in the outhouse. No one cared. Bethany open a beer and said David would be back. I didn't understand and tried to explain that we should leave on foot. Katie wouldn't listen, refused to go without Neal. The whole thing was insane, and unfortunately I started screaming about the woods being evil. That just made Katie cry harder.

Everything that happened next is somewhat hazy. Lucy handed me some pills, told me to take them. They weren't my usual medications, but I trusted her. Bethany soothed Katie and Lucy poured tequila down my throat. I knew this was all a horrible idea, but soon I didn't care. I remember music, and the girls dancing. At some point I burnt myself trying to cook some of the steak that David had brought. Later, I threw up that steak. Hours flew by in a drunken blur. Katie was crying again, and I was trying to get Lucy's clothes off. I think Lucy and I had sex, while Katie screamed.

Katie screamed while she was on fire.

I was on my back in the grass, watching as Bethany and Lucy pranced naked around the fire. What was left of Katie was in the flames, curled and charred. Or were those the rest of the logs? Where was Katie? I turned my head and gazed out into the woods. There, hundreds of people stood among the trees, their eyes shining in reverence. Worshipping eyes, acolyte eyes. The sanctity of madness, consecrated in violence. I took these to be the citizens of McKinley, here to observe whatever ritual they had set in motion, Bethany and Lucy chosen as their new priestesses.

The glow from the flames as they drank from the bottle and poured it over each other, licking the tequila from each other's skin. Between laughter, they spoke in a language, guttural and cruel. The earth rumbled. I stirred and gawked over my shoulder in direction of the outhouse. Something large was coming, making wet, sucking sounds as it pulled its way up the incline.

Lucy knelt down beside me. "I always loved you."

What sounded like someone clearing their throat, but a thousand times louder blasted me to unconsciousness.

There was this brief, fragmented memory of waking up in the morning, face down in the grass. Reality was soft around the edges, and not to be trusted. I knew that it was all a façade, my shattered mind piecing together a comfortable illusion.

The truck was back, and David was passed out in its bed. Taking a few steps towards him, I tripped over something that elicited a groan. Lucy and Bethany were sprawled out on the ground, clothed and passed out. Just then Neal popped his head out of one of the Adirondacks.

"Hey man, what's going on?"

I began screaming.

I was found roaming the highway, most of my cognitive facilities impaired. That was three months ago. Everyone else is still missing. Because of my history of mental illness, I'm being blamed.

The authorities say we never went to McKinley, that we reserved a campsite at a different park. Supposedly McKinley doesn't even have campsites. Maybe I got the name wrong, but I know I could show them the place.

There're all these theories. Most people think I killed them, but I know I didn't hurt anyone. I couldn't have. I keep demanding proof, asking where the bodies are. The doctors throw out all these terms and the cops just want me to be up locked up. My own parents refuse to speak to me.

I've sat here in this room, agonizing over what did or didn't actually happen up there in those woods for weeks. The drugs they're filling me with keep me calm, but don't help me remember. I understand my story is insane, but that doesn't mean parts of it aren't true. I did *not* kill them, and if I didn't kill them, where the hell are they?

I want to know what happened to my wife and brother. What happened to my friends. I just want to know what really happened.

I did not kill them.

❧ 7 ☙

GLIMPSE OF DULL KNIVES

"WE CAN'T STAY HERE," said the old man.

Declan glanced up from the engine and frowned. He was well aware of their situation. No one chose to break down in the valley.

"We'll be running again soon," he replied.

He had six passengers in the caravan this time. Six was manageable, but it didn't pay much. At least two of them looked like they could handle a gun if trouble arose, maybe even that kid, too. Not that guns would help much if Skullings came.

"Momma, is that a dead god?" asked the boy.

"Hush now, you know better. That was not one of our gods."

Declan peered up the side of the hill at the enormous, mummified corpse sprawled out across the land. It was easily a mile long and had laid there for a century, if the stories could be believed. It was a remnant of the Threshold War, and a relatively benign sight considering what else one could see these days.

The Alusian Merchant came running up to him, waving something above his head. "I found it!"

"Good, that's good," said Declan. "That will make this all go a lot faster."

He took the part from the merchant and connected it into the engine. The bypass distributor was technically illegal on a transport like this, but it was either that or be stuck out in the valley after dark. Chances were few of them would have survived.

"I'll pay you for the part as soon as we arrive in Yulsa, Sir," said Declan.

"My name is Yassin. And please, no worries," said the merchant. "My life is more valuable than seventy-five bit."

Declan nodded and gestured for everyone to get back into to the transport wagon. Behind it, another wagon carried their belongings, assorted cargo, and private packages for discrete transport. Both were vaguely rectangular shaped with curved tops and heavily armored. The hover-mags beneath kept them lifted nearly four feet off the ground at all times, the duty of Declan's small thermal tug to move them along.

Everyone aboard, he locked the cargo with the keypad and a fingerprint scan. The same could be done with the passengers if they didn't unlock their wagon from the inside. Climbing back inside his tug, he fired up its engines and began the pull. There was always an initial moment of resistance, but then they began to move. Passage like this wasn't fast, but once they got moving, they could reach a steady pace of forty-five MHP. Slow, but safe out here.

Aiming the tug, he turned away to do some quick calculations on his Servant-8. The old cybernetic interface told him they should just make it out of the valley before nightfall. Just barely. He kept both of his guns charged and nearby.

The valley appeared green and beautiful. Thick grass, colorful wildflowers, and even a few trees on the north side. You had to ignore the dead giant, of course. In reality, it was a death trap, home to monstrosities lurking underground. Supposedly, the world was different once, long ago, centuries before the Threshold War. Everything used to be something else. Declan understood that.

The intercom in the tug buzzed. "We're having trouble getting a signal out of Yulsa."

Declan checked his connections. "Everything is fine on my end. Must be Yulsa."

There was some grumbling. "Okay, thank you."

Declan rolled his eyes. He used to be a caravan driver providing transport and protection for said transport, and that was it. Now, he was expected to shell out for food, blankets, and even signal boosters. This group hadn't been that bad, but he'd had some a few weeks back he'd almost dumped in the Texxa desert. Their entitlement had been staggering.

In the end, he hadn't dumped them. He'd killed enough people in his life. He safely deposited them in Oleans like they wanted and then he got drunk. He must have said something to a few of the patrons while hammered, because when he saw two of his passengers the next day, they ran from him. They must have been informed who their tug driver was.

It wasn't a memory Declan liked to dwell on. He didn't want to be anyone. Not anymore.

The tug kept moving and they made their way out of the valley, slightly ahead of the schedule Declan had predicted. Not a Skulling sighted. The valley grew flat and more barren, the grass dispersing. There were sparse outcroppings of rubble here and there, remnants of a past world. Some of these were still used by scavengers and squatters, none of whom had ever bothered Declan in his travels. These building had long ago collapsed, rusted and eroded, much like the people who huddled within them.

He spotted a handful of people in the distance. Declan moved his handgun closer, then realized who he was seeing. The Order of Secretion. A religious group that sought enlightenment through sexual acts; they had never posed a threat to anyone.

There were about a dozen of them. As he passed, the lead woman raised her hand in greeting, her robe open to reveal her naked form beneath. Declan waved back, hoping they weren't heading for the valley.

It was a few hours later when he could make out the lighthouse in Yulsa. The beacon shone straight up into the air, a bluish-white beam that could be seen for miles in every direction. He had wanted to make the city by nightfall, but the engine problems had knocked him off by about five hours. Chances were, he would be expected to knock fifty bits off everyone's fare.

The line at the gate was worrisome. Technically, the Yulsa authorities had no jurisdiction outside the wall and bandits often took advantage of that. They were far less courageous during the day, but now issues were an inevitability.

Sure enough, they had only moved one vehicle ahead when there came a knocking on the side of his door.

Declan glance over to see a toothless man grinning up at him, a few muscular bruisers standing behind. There only looked to be four of them, but then he heard a knock from the other side of his cab. Another handful. One of them glowed in the light of a plasma torch.

He gave them a wave to back away from the door an opened it. "How can I help you gentleman?"

Toothless brushed back his long, stringy hair. "Evenin' Driver! If you was unaware, it's quite perilous on this here road to Yulsa. My compatriots and I would be more that agreeable to ensure your safe passage for a small fee."

Of course. "I carry no money for such a transaction, friend. All goods are locked up tight until our arrival in Yulsa."

"Highly unfortunate," he said, sucking on his gums. "Perhaps if we was to ask your passengers?"

Declan sighed. "I don't think so."

The men from the other side of the cab had come around to gather with their boss. Only two of them had guns, but the rest were armed with an assortment of melee weapons like hatchets and clubs. Oh, and the guy lugging the torch around. Eleven in all it looked like. More than he had thought.

"We'll be speaking to them passengers now," said Toothless.

Those guns would have to go first.

Damn everything.

Declan whipped out his pistol and fired twice. Headshots dropped the two before the assembled thugs even knew what had happened. Swinging his rifle off his shoulder, he aimed for the plasma torch housing unit and pulled the trigger. It exploded, taking out the guy who had been carrying it and a couple of the men standing beside it. In five seconds, eleven had gone down to six.

Toothless began screaming, about to attack, but it didn't matter. Declan allowed his rifle to swing back to his shoulder and pulled a sunblade from its sheathe off his legs. He waded into the men with it and his pistol. He sliced and shot, making quick work of them. Their screams died quickly, leaving only Toothless to bleed out in the dirt.

The little gang boss lay there clutching the gaping hole his in his stomach, trying to scurry away. Declan walked up and shot him in the head before he had a chance to say anything. Ignoring the wide-eyed stares from his passengers, he picked up a few items of use of the ground and tossed them into the cab.

Finished, he climbed back in and moved them forward. Absently, he reached down and caressed the face of his watch. A pre-Threshold relic, it had never worked, but it meant the world to him.

Entry at the gate ended up going smoothly. Maybe this guard shift was easy going, maybe they knew what he had done on the road and didn't want any extra problems. Hell, they could've been pleased he had done them a service. Declan didn't care what the reason was, he only wanted this ride over. Papers scanned, he pulled them into port and unlocked both transports.

None of the passengers would look him in the eyes as they disembarked, only quietly thanking him as they went to gather their things. None asked for a refund. Everything that wasn't a piece of passenger's property was placed into a storage shed with a biometric lock. Declan was done with his cargo and securing his tug, when he found a few of his passengers still loitering around.

The Alusian Merchant, Yassin, along with the old man, and a pretty young woman dressed in expensive clothes. He had a notion she was from one of the lower Noble Houses, but hadn't cared enough to asked. He noticed the woman peer over again as the old man strolled towards him.

"My name is Rugan. We would like to thank you for what you did on the road. Allow us to buy you a drink."

Declan shook his head. "It was part of my job."

"Aye," said Rugan. "Then allow one former Marshall to buy another a drink. We won't tell the others."

Declan head snapped around to catch Rugan subtly tap his chest twice and motion two fingers towards his forehead. It was the salute of the Noram Marshalls, the independent paladin sect of the continent. To falsify such credentials was a death sentence.

Declan nodded. "Between us. I know a place."

The tavern might have had a name, but no one knew it because it didn't have a sign. The alcohol was cheap, the food was mediocre, and the tables were perpetually sticky. Regardless, Declan had never run into trouble inside its walls, security about the only thing taken seriously there.

As soon as they entered, a tiny, cybernetically enhanced woman pounced on Declan. "My gloomy man! Where have you been?"

"I've been working, Ying."

She eyed the others. "Who are these wonderful people?"

"Passengers."

"You bring passengers to my establishment? Fantastic! Trevor, free blooming plates for Gloomy and his friends! You're buying your own drinks."

Yassin took her hand. "My dear, you are a vision of beauty and commerce."

They left the two flirting and found a table. A young man came out and deposited four round baskets before standing there impatiently for their drink orders. The young noble seemed terribly confused, so Declan ordered ales for everyone.

"I'm sorry, this is all very new to me," she said.

"It's fine."

"Such rudeness, forgive me. My name Noelle San-Octario Velize. Uh, just call me Noelle."

"Noelle it is."

"Mr. Declan," she said, pointing down to her blooming plate. "What is this?"

"It's an old pre-Threshold dish. The outer portions are potatoes that have been sliced, fried, and seasoned. They're called French Fries. The inner sections are similar but made from onions. Onion Rings. You add extra flavor with that dipping sauce in the center. It all goes very good with beer, very tasty."

Noelle tried a French Fry and her eyes lit up. "So simple, but so delicious!"

Yassin sauntered over to the table, smiling. "I think I will be coming back here."

Declan saw Ying making eyes at the distinguished merchant. Knowing her, she was already plotting marriage. Poor guy.

It was a strange collection of people at the table, and Declan was already beginning to feel uncomfortable. He hadn't engaged in much social interaction the past five years. Any glimmer of light in his life sent him spiraling.

Yassin raised a glass. "Shall we toast to our valiant driver?"

There it was, that hollowness in his bones. That coldness. Declan closed his eyes and wished away the world. This had been a mistake.

"Lower your glass," said Rugan. "We are not here for revelry."

"We're not?"

"No. We are thanking Mr. Declan by paying for his food and drink, that is all. Perhaps some company in the dark of night. He did his job, and we should be happy of that."

Noelle nodded. "And I am thankful of that, sir. This is my first appointment, an ambassadorship here to Yulsa. I am the youngest of my House, and I do believe I am expected to fail. I hope to disappoint those holding such beliefs."

"Good for you, dear!" said Yassin, wolfing down a mouthful of onion rings. "I'm here to open another trading portal. It would make my eighth! Very exciting times, indeed! What of you, Mr. Rugan?"

"I am in my retirement and simply traveling."

"What did you used to do?"

Rugan and Declan exchanged looks, Declan giving him a slight nod.

"I was a Marshall."

Both Yassin and Noelle sat up straighter, a French Fry halfway to Noelle's mouth.

"Are… are you serious?" she asked.

"It's an Executive Termination Crime to impersonate a Marshall, living, retired, or deceased," replied Rugan.

Noelle bowed her head. "Your Governance, we, we didn't know!"

"I'm just Rugan now, child. There's no need for that. I left The Knot to live free in my final years."

Yassin gestured for more ale. "But why?"

"Leave him be," said Declan.

"It's alright. I gave my time to the Marshalls, now I wanted some time to myself. Does that make sense?"

Both Yassin and Noelle appeared to try and tumble this around their skulls. Declan looked straight at the old man, raised his cup slightly, and tilted it towards him. Rugan nodded, and did the same back.

They continued eating, trying to keep the conversation from straying back to Rugan's past. It didn't work, and he ended up answering about a dozen questions over the next two hours. Declan found himself in a strange state where he wasn't uncomfortable nor actually happy with this situation he found himself in, simply resigned to it. If anything, there was a certain sort of solace knowing Rugan existed. He found his fingers straying to his watch.

Declan was on his fourth beer when Ying came up to the table with a strange look on her face. "I didn't… I hadn't realized what day it was when you came it earlier. I'm sorry. I always hope you won't be here when it comes."

"It's today?" he said, standing up.

"Yes."

Declan looked to the table. "Thank you. I must leave."

He went to rush out then stop. He turned back and gave Rugan the formal salute of the Marshalls. Rugan saluted back, and Declan was gone.

"Wait, what was that?" asked Noelle.

Ying narrowed her eyes at Rugan. "You are as he is?"

"I am retired Marshall Sebastian Rugan, Second Class. I know who that man is, and I believe I know what he is about to do."

Ying nodded curtly. "Tell them."

"Our tug driver, Mr. Declan, is in fact one Declan Thames."

Yassin leaned back in his chair and covered his mouth in shocked, but Noelle simply shrugged. "Who's that?"

"Former Marshall Declan Thames, First Class. He and his partner Brandon Erring were the most efficient and decorate team in the history of The Knot. Then Erring was killed fighting a religious order that worshipped one of the remaining Titans. Even though they were clearly guilty of human trafficking and sexually slavery, The Marshalls became embroiled in legalities over their religious freedoms. Freedoms for rapists and slave traders. Declan Thames went rogue, and took care of it himself."

"What do you mean?" asked Noelle.

"Brandon Erring was more than his partner by the standards of The Knot. He was Declan's husband. So Declan went in and slaughtered all one hundred and sixty-five members of the cult in one night. Even though he had many supporters, and likely could've returned had he prostrated himself before The Knot, something had broke inside him. He was denounced and banished."

"My god, that's all so horrible," said Noelle. "But where is he going now?"

Ying frowned. "Where else? To slay the Titan that started this all."

FOR FIVE YEARS, he had been trying to find someone who had been able to map her path. Zigging and zagging across the continent, constantly changing speeds, it was almost impossible for anyone outside of government resources to plot her course. Eventually, he had discovered a scholar who had deduced the Titan's movements were not random. She was following a very complex, but set trail.

Ying believed he was here to engage the Titan, but that would not be this particular morning. No, as the sun rose today, he was here only to watch her pass. To see The Ruined Princess with his own eyes and attempt to understand.

He had paid off one of the guards a ridiculous amount to borrow his skiff. Racing over eight miles outside of Yulsa, he found the coordinates the old scholar had given him. Parking, he looked around and saw nothing. Climbing up a rocky ledge, he peered over into a wide ravine. It took him a moment to realize what he was starring into.

It was a groove worn into the earth, the path of Izzika. The Ruined Princess.

Across from him, the sun began to peek up from the horizon. As the illumination seeped out into the dark sky, another light gleamed from the north. This one was blue, smaller and sharper.

Every day since Brandon had died, there had been an ache inside him. It hadn't been soothed by the obliteration of the cult, only consuming what was left of him as the days had gone by. His partner, his best friend, his husband, -- in place of all that now just a void. He knew Brandon would be disappointed at what he'd become, pissed at his reckless mission of vengeance, but he didn't have anything else. The Knot had been his home and Brandon his family, but both were gone now.

As the sun rose higher, Izzika drew closer.

Declan pulled up a pair of binoculars. The devastation she left in her wake was as the legends said. Something like blades leapt from the ground, forged from the very minerals of the earth. Still white-hot and flaming blue, they reared up at precarious angles, jutting from the dirt. Some appeared average in size, but most were massive, the size of buildings. Thousands blossomed at her footfalls, swords reaching for the sky instead of flowers.

He had been prepared for this sight, but not so much for Izzika herself. After all that had happened, Declan had conjured images of a beast. A slavering creature who took glee in the wreckage she caused.

The Ruined Princess appeared as a young girl. It was hard to determine such thing as age, but a young teenager, perhaps. A darker shade of skin, almost like Brandon, he thought with pain, but with long, thick white hair. She was naked, but at the same time, clothed in the blue flames that danced along the blades. Her small face was placid, almost...

... sad.

Declan sat on the ledge and watched her pass. She never looked his way or acknowledged him in any fashion. The weaponry erupted behind her, trailing back for miles until it slowly dissipated into small protrusions. Within hours, the flames would go out, and then in a few days the swords, stakes, and pikes would crumble back into their natural state without her power to compel them.

"Like any natural disaster, her coming brings great strife, but her stay is only temporary."

That's what the scholar had told him. He had dismissed his words at the time, only concerned with revenge. Kill the Titan or die trying.

Declan ran his fingers along the face of the watch. Brandon had found it and had it inscribed on the back. *Love as Strong as Us.* His husband had been the strongest person he'd ever known, a far better man than Declan.

He lay back on the ledge and stared up into the brightening sky. High above, something shot through the clouds and left a plume of red energy in its wake. It glimmered for a few moments before casting the surrounding area into a pink hue. Nothing remarkable, nothing dangerous.

Declan realized he had been holding his breathe. He exhaled.

❧ 8 ☙

PALE REMAINS OF ROYALTY

IF YOU'VE DRIVEN down a single stretch of any state route in semi-rural Ohio for a decent length of time, you've seen all of semi-rural Ohio. It all looks the same, especially if it's in March. Sure, there are some metropolitan centers scattered here and there, desperately clinging onto whatever culture and sophistication they can find, but mostly it's the opposite of urbane. As the snow still melts, leaving everything wet and gray, the truth is apparent. We are muddy fields hoping for growth and big rigs parked askew, houses built on hollow dreams and road kill, billboards offering empty salvation and irrational loyalty to sports teams far away.

We are the future, strangled by the hands of our home.

I was still getting ready when Mackenzie showed up. It was easy enough to hear her talking to my mom downstairs while I finished putting on makeup. The makeup was nothing more than an issue of vanity, maybe insecurity, but it made me feel better. Enough to be standing next to Mackenzie. Checking my face in the mirror, and fingers through my hair, I grabbed my purse and headed downstairs.

Laughing with my mom, Mackenzie glanced over and stuck her tongue out at me. Beautiful and funny, she was also as poor as me. The only reason she had a car was because her mom had gotten injured at work. The whole situation was a mess. Mackenzie now worked part-time at that shithole diner in town to help out her family.

Mackenzie made another wisecrack, and my mom chuckled into her hand. It was just my mom and I, no one else. She had worked at the dog food factory for fifteen years. It had kept a roof over our heads, but that was about it. Even though I had a 3.8 GPA and was due to graduate in a couple months, there were concerns about money for tuition, even with scholarships and grants. This was reality.

"You ready?" I asked.

"You girls have a good time, and be safe," said my mom. "What movie are you seeing?"

Mackenzie shrugged. "Eh, we'll figure it out when we all get there."

Good save. We weren't going to the movies.

We climbed into the beat up Pontiac Vibe that Mackenzie drove and headed out. I wanted to ask her some questions about tonight, but she cranked up the stereo. It could wait. Singing badly, we roared down the street.

It's not that I hated my life, or even my hometown, necessarily. It was simply when I critically examined it, all I came away with was despair. You need to understand that. I didn't see a way out, not a simple one. Not a sane one. None of us did. We decided on an insane one.

We pulled up in front of Eliza's house, where she was waiting for us with Jocelyn. I had been friends with Mackenzie and Eliza for years, but didn't know Jocelyn all that well. Eliza was in almost the exact same situation as me, but Jocelyn made us all look like royalty. Pretty in a tomboyish kind of way, I had heard she'd been homeless a few times. No one deserved that, especially a kid.

After they were in the car, Mackenzie turned the music down. "I'm guessing everybody is still onboard for this?"

"I don't buy a word of it," said Jocelyn. "But it's worth a shot."

"And you're sure you know where we're going?" I asked.

Mackenzie laughed. "Yeah, I'm sure."

About three weeks ago, Lillian Moore had returned to her hometown for surveying. A multi-million dollar land developer out west now, she still remained a beloved daughter of the area. Moore had shaken hands and kissed babies before stopping in at a local diner for another short publicity shoot. While she was there, something about Mackenzie had caught her eye. After all the cameras had stopped, Moore had caught her out back sneaking a cigarette.

According to Moore, she had received a little help rising to her current station. Another white trash Ohio girl with no prospects, she had run into a famous lawyer who told her about a barn. It was her turn to return the favor. Mackenzie had been filled in on all the details, who in turn told all of us.

Eliza shifted her slight frame up in the seat. "I'm still a little hazy here. This ritual or whatever only works for women, and there has to be four of us?"

"I guess so," said Mackenzie.

"And we're asking to become rich and famous?"

"That sounds about right."

Eliza glanced over at me. "If you say so."

"I dunno if I'm down for sacrificing chickens or any shit like that," said Jocelyn, crossing her arms.

Mackenzie had been vague on what exactly we were expected to do to achieve these goals. I didn't know if she wasn't entirely clear, or if she was holding back information, worried we'd back out. Looking back, I'm still not sure. I only knew what this meant to me.

I *didn't* know what to think about everyone in the car. Eliza was obviously dubious, and Jocelyn acted like she didn't want to be there. Mackenzie seemed to think it was all an adventure, and that frustrated me. Made me think the whole thing might be a joke. I wouldn't have put it past her. I could understand Eliza's attitude, but I couldn't wrap my head around Jocelyn. Wouldn't you try anything to make life better, to escape hopelessness?

Apparently the barn was a little over forty miles north from us. Eliza and Jocelyn fell into whispering in the back seat, while Mackenzie turned the stereo back on. Fiddling with her aux cord, she selected a playlist with everything and cranked up the volume. The outside world zoomed past, dreariness enveloping the trees and houses. Rusted cars sitting outside trailers that looked barely livable, yards filled with tacky and sun-faded decorations, feral children covered in bruises and dirt screaming at the sky, businesses with windows boarded up and names already forgotten, more farm equipment sitting in empty fields than I could care to count. Tiny towns of no consequence just like ours, all connected by a color that should be green.

Leaning forward, Eliza asked me about an assignment in history. We had shared all the same classes since middle school; Eliza was another overachiever seeking passage out of here through grades. She was sweet, but we didn't have much in common other than that. I suppose you could say she was more Disney pop to my anime alternative. It's these interests of mine that kept Mackenzie and I bonded.

A secret black magic ritual in an abandoned barn. Yeah, Mackenzie would've been into that as soon as Moore said the words.

We turned off down a road that looked like it hadn't been used in decades, weeds sprouting up between the tire ruts. None of us spoke, and I hadn't noticed the music being turned off at some point. We were about an hour away from dusk, and the landscape looked leeched of color. Whatever had grown here once had given way to wispy strands of tall, sickly-looking grass blowing in the wind.

A lone tree on the land had died at some point and

collapsed into the small house on the property. It had crushed the roof, scattering shingles. All of the windows had been broken, and the paint was faded beyond recognition. Even the concrete slab that acted as a porch had weathered and begun to crumble. The door, possibly taken off its hinges, lay in the yard, leaving the house open to the elements.

We passed it, eyes wide, down a short decline to the barn.

The barn was in slightly better shape. Its traditional red had aged to a brown reminiscent of dried blood. The whole two-story structure seemed to lean, as if the support beams were slowly rotting. Its doors were still intact, cracked open wide enough to let a person slip inside. There were a few pine trees off in the distance behind the barn, but other than them, there was nothing else to see for miles. No other additional buildings, no farm equipment, and no signs of life.

Mackenzie parked in front of the barn. "We're here."

"How did you even find this place?" I asked. "You didn't use you GPS or anything."

"Sure I did," she replied. "When I came out here the first time a couple days ago."

"What?"

She gave me a look. "I wasn't going to drag you guys around on a wild goose chase if I didn't check it all out to make sure it was legit first."

Eliza and Jocelyn seemed to find that quite reasonable, but it made me anxious. I wouldn't have cared if she had scouted out the location first, but she hadn't told any of us. What else hadn't she told us? Maybe I was being paranoid, but I read once that it paid to be paranoid. Paranoia kept you alive, and naivety got you dead.

For a minute or two, we all peered up at the barn. It was intimidating, in ways that are hard to describe. It wasn't just old and creepy, it had a presence. There was a reverence here, almost like a church, yet unnatural. It gave me a certain sense of longing for something, something I had never known I had lost. I can't say it was evil exactly, not sinister or malicious, but unnerving.

Mackenzie coughed and shook her head. "Let's go."

Inside, the light was dim and filtered through the warped slats of the barn walls. It smelled deeply of turned earth and rotting hay. From what I could see, everything had been cleaned out of the barn, leaving a large space below; plus whatever may have been hiding above in the rafters. It was silent, not even the sound of scurrying rats or buzzing insects. The only thing that appeared out of place was a small mound of dirt in the center of the barn that looked recently made.

"Okay, now what?" asked Eliza, looking around.

Mackenzie went to the mound and started digging. I was about to ask her what she was doing when she pulled out a wooden box about nine-by-six inches. It was plain, but heavily varnished. Opening it, she pulled out a small book that looked ancient.

"This was exactly where Lillian Moore said it would be. I checked it out, read through it, and put it back," she said.

I came up behind Mackenzie. "What's it say?"

"Not much. It's a journal dated 1908. Only one person wrote in it and she never gave her name."

"Read it out loud," Eliza said to Mackenzie, shooting me a glance.

I knew what that meant. There was a reason I was looking over her shoulder.

Mackenzie flipped to the front and began.

"November 14th, 1908

"I commit this to paper with the knowledge there can be but two outcomes for me. By the end of this night I shall either have found a new fate for myself, or found death by my own hand. No longer can I endure this life, suffering every day under father's mistreatments, no end in sight.

"Annabelle, Helen, and Mary all feel as I do. Once united in our misery, we have found a possible solution. In cleaning for Mr.

Morrison, did Mary come upon one of his many arcane tomes. This one contained a most Un-Christian ceremony for women, one that claims to grant kindly favors. It is simple and requires four women.

"We have already sanctified the earth within my family's barn with the blood from womanly flow, and blood retrieved from our fathers."

"Hell, do we have to throw used tampons on the ground?" asked Jocelyn.

"No, we don't," said Mackenzie. "Let me finish."

"Tonight we will proceed, tonight I shall be free."

"Is that it?" asked Eliza.

"Nope," said Mackenzie, as she turned the page.

"The ceremony was not as I expected, but it was a success. The land has been forever marked by what we have done. I have been instructed to leave this journal here for those in the future who might wish to seek out the ravenous lower entity who grants these boons. Additional blood is unneeded, but the incantation that I will copy down on the next page is. Four women must stand in four corners and state their names in supplication, then one must read the aloud the final page. I am told this will be sufficient.

"For those who follow, find strength. It is worth it."

We were all struck silent. What do you say to something like that?

"I'm not real thrilled with the 'ravenous lower entity' part of that story," said Eliza.

Mackenzie snorted. "What would a bunch of good little religious girls know at the turn of the century?"

"What, you think we're about to ring up an alien?" I asked.

"This place is freaking me out," said Jocelyn, examining the rafters. "If we're going to do it, can we just get it done?"

We took our places, each of us about eight feet away from the mound and lining up with the walls of the barn. There was some discussion about positioning, but we decided it didn't matter. Eliza wondered if we should recite our full names, and the rest of us agreed that was probably for the best. Mackenzie proclaimed she was going to be the one to read the incantation. Nobody complained, but I was holding my tongue. I suppose part of me didn't trust her in all of this.

Mackenzie began, stating her full name clearly, and then we all followed, going around. When it got back to her, she looked down to the journal and read the lines written there. The words were pretty in a strange way. It occurred to me that Mackenzie was likely butchering the pronunciations. She had failed Spanish, so the chances of her speaking an unknown language with any fluency were pretty slim. The realization began to set in that this was all likely some kind of prank, either played by my friend or by Moore for some reason.

Then the light in the barn began to change.

At first I thought a cloud was simply passing overhead, the illumination slipping through the siding growing dim. But the shadows grew thicker, heavier. The thin blades of light were choked out by the darkness, and I heard one of the other girls scream. Even the door was gone.

I heard Mackenzie yell out, "Don't move!"

The darkness was complete and full. More than that, it had weight. I could feel it surrounding me, touching me. Then, there in that deeper black, I sensed something move in front of me. The heaviness began to recede, the shadows broken again once more by the light streaming through the dilapidated barn walls.

A young woman stood on the mound in the center of us.

I think Eliza screamed, I don't know. I was too busy staring in awe. The girl looked to be our age, seventeen or eighteen. Stunningly beautiful with pale skin and light blue eyes. She had white hair that hung somewhat disheveled past her shoulders, with a silver filigree crown askew on her head. Barefoot on the mound, she wore an immaculate white dress. The material looked somehow organic, as if it was alive. I would've been moved to say she looked like an angel.

Except instead of feathered wings, she was covered in spiders.

Hundreds of spiders, all different kinds.

"What the fuck are you?" asked Eliza.

She turned and smiled at Eliza. My friend had collapsed onto the ground, and Jocelyn looked ready to bolt out of the doors. Mackenzie clutched the journal to her chest and smiled manically.

"I am possibility," the girl on the mound sang.

Her voice was amazing, sensual yet comforting. It elicited responses emotional and physical. I felt it in my heart and between my legs, driving me forward and calming me down.

I couldn't help it, I had to know. "Please, what's your name?"

She sang a short aria that caused my body to tremble. Finishing, she held up her hands as if to gesture that was all the answer I was going to get. Two spiders fell off her fingers and skittered back up onto her leg.

"We summoned you to make our lives better," said Mackenzie. "For 'kindly favors,' like you gave other women in the past. That's what we were told."

"I know. All true," sang the girl on the mound.

"Oh, Okay. Cool," replied Mackenzie.

We all looked at each other. I don't think any of us believed this could be really happening, that it could've been real. I had hoped, but I hadn't been willing to invest too much into that hope. I know Eliza and Jocelyn hadn't.

I almost started crying at the idea. Escaping the area, fleeing ongoing poverty and teen pregnancy, economic hardship and ingrained misogyny. It wasn't about fame and fortune, it was about fulfillment. No matter what anyone wanted to admit, eighteen year old girls didn't have the same opportunities as boys the same age. Not around here. We were told to be quiet, hurry up and have babies by the time you were twenty, so you could get hooked on drugs and die.

We all must have been lost in our own thoughts, because the girl on the mound was humming. The tune was unknown to me, but it was gorgeous. Perhaps we had all been lulled into a trance because of it, given a chance to consider who we were and want we wanted. Looking back, that's likely the case.

Mackenzie was still gripping ahold of the journal protectively. "So what has to happen here? What do you have to do?"

"I give my blessings," sang the girl on the mound. "Once the devotee is chosen."

Eliza climbed to her feet. "What does that mean?"

"One steps forward and says they are most worthy, leaving her sisters to be sacrificed."

"You can't…" started Mackenzie.

I didn't even hesitate. "I'm the most worthy. I'll be your devotee."

The others gawked at me. Shocked. Terrified.

I think Mackenzie swore at me, I don't know. My eyes never waivered from the girl on the mound. She smiled back at me.

"So bold," she sang to me.

The darkness began to encroach once again. Jocelyn tried to make for the barn doors, but they where gone before she could reach them. I heard her screams and wet splashing, something being dragged off into the corner. Somehow still lit from an unseen source, I kept my sight locked on the girl on the mound. I couldn't stop what I glimpsed in my peripheral though.

The darkness was alive with monsters. Spiders, but far larger, far more grotesque. Turned inside out, and rebuilt with other, less comprehensible parts. They moved like horrifying black stars, twinkling and twitching and they made their way throughout what I allowed myself to still see of the barn, what I allowed myself to see of Eliza and Mackenzie.

Both of them had been overcome by the spiders. Eliza hadn't lasted long, her head torn off and the creatures crawling in and out of her body, feeding or nesting. Mackenzie fought longer, swatting the away with the journal. Finally the shadows consumed her, followed by a sickening crunch. Her hand fell into what light the girl on the mound threw across the dark space, before it was pulled back, never to be seen again.

"They will suffice," she sang.

"And me?"

Stepping off the mound, she walked towards me. I stiffened, terrified of what to expect. Standing in front of me, she lifted the spider-infested crown off her head and went to place it on mine. I said nothing, didn't even make a face, but inside I was shrieking.

The crown rested upon me and I saw everything.

I saw my future, how it would play out. Luck would turn in my favor from here on out, anytime I needed it to. I would be happy and successful. I would be fulfilled. At forty-two, I would return to the town nearby my own and pass the information of the barn onto another teenage girl. I saw her face.

The vision faded and I saw that the barn was empty and normal except for the girl on the mound, the crown back on her head.

"Now what?" I asked.

She leaned up and kissed my forehead. "Live."

Her body broke apart into a million spiders and they disappeared off into the dwindling light of the barn. It had gotten late, and dusk had passed into the edge of night. I walked over and picked up the journal, dusted it off and placed it back in the wooden box before burying it in the mound again.

By the mound, I found Mackenzie's car keys. I knew she had them in her purse, so I took that as a sign that the luck was truly working in my favor. I wasn't entirely sure what I was going to do next, but I knew it would work out for me. And it did. I won't bother going into any of those details, but everyone believed the story that was concocted. It's why I don't worry about writing all this down.

You see, I wasn't given luck. Luck is fleeting and fickle.

I was given possibilities.

All you have to do is be willing to seize them.

❊ *9* ❊

A DIRGE EVERENDING

IF YOU'RE READING THIS, hopefully we pulled it off. If not, well at least you'll die knowing the truth. Forgive me if my writing seems disjointed, as I'm still getting used to some things.

UP ON THE HILL, I watched as a creature made of shadows and legs tore apart a school. The school had been empty for a month, but it still bothered me. I'd seen too many dead kids so far this past year.

"That's a big one," said Zoe.

Jamison grunted. "Makes it more fun. You know you love it."

"You're right. Bitches love monsters."

It took a lot to suppress an eye roll. Instead, I squatted down and touched my fingertips to the ground. Senses spread out and took everything in. It was a type of situational aware-ness. Spatial understanding, probability calculating, a touch of clairvoyance. I could fight well enough, but this is was how I worked best in the field.

"See that bright spot in its center mass?" I said pointing down at the creature. "That's where we need to hit."

Jamison reached out into the aether and retrieved a massive war hammer. "Consider it done."

Before I could say anything else, Zoe called up her powers and launched him into the air. Jamison sailed easily a quarter mile through the night sky with the hammer raised over his head, ready for battle. I couldn't make out what he bellowed out as he had soared off.

Zoe and I slid down the hill, feeling the impact of his strike the same time we heard it. It wasn't a physical blow, but a spiritual one. Scientists would say bio-electrical energies colliding. The big brains still argued over it. Mana, Chi, Prana, it had many names. Collectively, we had come to call it Gias.

Jamison had damaged the creature badly, but it wasn't dead yet. Tentacle-like limbs flailed as it diminished in size, the darkness inside itself shifting to conceal its core. It had no true form, no real shape outside of a hazy idea. The dim light Jamison had struck was its concept being born, something they couldn't allow.

A limb writhed in my direction. I quickly sliced off the end with my katana, more to investigate the severed piece than to protect myself. It felt like a giant worm that had been left out in the sun. Still, my senses told me what I needed.

"Jamison, keep at that spot!" I yelled. "Zoe, box it in."

Zoe pulled back her attack, blew the short black bangs out her face, and nodded. She began to concentrate on a mental structure as Jamison whaled away with his hammer. The two couldn't have looked any more different in the face of battle at that moment. One in a state of contemplative grace, with the other laughing madly.

The tentacles had begun to wither, the shadows dissipate. All those hits had caused the light to fade considerably. The creature was barely formed to begin with, and hadn't enough sentient thought to protect itself from Jamison, lashing out at those on the ground instead. It hadn't developed into a full Wight yet. Because of that, it was almost over now.

"Get clear," I called up.

Jamison leapt off the creature, clearly breaking his leg in the fall, but was healed in the next step with a burst of Gias energy. A reckless move, but one I didn't have time to worry about just then.

Although there was still a flicker of life within, it didn't matter. Zoe had finished her cage, and it was time to draw it smaller. The walls closed in, crushing the creature from all six sides. It went from the size of a garage to the size of a dice, floating there in the air. Its light extinguished, the only thing inside now was power.

It floated over to Zoe's hand, a tiny cube that radiated blue-black energy. She opened her satchel and took out a box approximately the dimensions of a cigarette box. Flipping open the lid, she slid the cube inside with a satisfied smile.

"Why do you get to keep the trophies?" asked Jamison.

"Because I'm the only one who can use them. Did you miss a meeting?"

"I'll have no sass from your sass mouth."

At this point, I did roll my eyes. "I'm leaving."

I'M ONLY CLEARED to say certain things. My name is Matsuda, and you don't need my first name. Before all this, I was a police detective in a major metropolitan city. That was two years ago, before the Wight Invasion.

The lunatic black guy is Jamison. All I know about him is that he used to be in Special Forces. That was more than I knew about Zoe, her background classified. We were all part of a Trinity Unit, comprised of people who had shown unique aptitude for harnessing Gias. All this Gias stuff kicked up the same time as the Wights showed up. There are a lot of theories, but nobody knows anything for sure.

To cut a long story short, the three of us ran around our sector and kicked the shit out of monsters with our super powers.

Zoe stared at the open refrigerator, swore loudly. The tall, slender twenty-something had showered and changed into sweat pants and a tank top. Her short black hair hung in a wet mess to her head.

"What's the matter, lollipop?" asked Jamison.

She looked back at us blankly. "Where's all the vodka?"

I paused with a slice of pizza halfway to my mouth. "You drank it all two days ago, remember?"

Zoe gave an exaggerated sigh. "Kids, do you know what happens when mommy doesn't get her special drink?"

I took the bite and chewed. Part of me worried about Zoe taking up alcoholism as a hobby, but it never seemed to affect her work. Honestly, even after downing more than half a bottle, she never seemed that hammered. It was weird.

"I don't want to hear you whine all night," said Jamison. "Top shelf on the left."

Eyes narrowed, she strolled across the kitchen and opened the cabinet. To her delight, she found a whole case of eighty proof moonshine.

Jamison summoned a squirt gun and fired it at her. "You get one bottle!"

"You're a goddamn prince, don't let Matsuda tell you otherwise!"

We really were some type of dysfunctional family. I had assumed the father role without any desire to do so, with these other two as the bickering children I never wanted. Jamison was openly gay. He told me once he was really picky and described his type by naming off a bunch off Hollywood actors I had never heard of. I got the impression they were all as large and aggressive as him. He hogged the television in all our down time. Zoe got flirty with me on occasion, but she could just as easily be distant and aloof. If she wasn't verbally sparring with Jamison, she was burning through ebooks on myriad topics. It was all very odd.

We all lived in a small converted warehouse. The living situation had been set up before the general public knew about the Wights, and there was a need for secrecy. We liked the place and it was centrally located, so we kept it when the curtain was pulled back. It worked out in the long run, because a number of more publicly known Trinity locations had been swarmed by refugees. Or attacked.

The later was far more disturbing when you considered the Wights could coordinate such a plan.

Zoe came back in from the kitchen and plopped down on one of the couches. She had a large glass with ice in it and nothing but clear liquid. Sipping it, she made a face.

"Are you drinking that straight?" I asked.

"No, I added a splash of Sprite for color."

"Yep, that sounds about right."

Jamison picked up a piece of pizza a frowned at it. "I wish more places were still open we could get food from. I'm getting sick of pizza."

"The Wight Invasion reminds me of the Covid pandemic," I said. "Some places are scared to open, others can't get employees to come in. We're in a decently urban area, and we have three pizza joints, two Asian places, a sub shop, and few fast food places that are mostly burgers. So don't complain too much."

Zoe laughed. "Don't forget the Mexican place."

"Yeah, the one that's only open for five hours in the middle of the day. That'll keep them safe somehow."

Jamison threw his half-eaten piece back into the box. "I miss hot wings."

———

ANOTHER CALL CAME IN.

A Wight had been spotted lurking in a parking garage near a business district. It was almost eighty miles away, so Zoe was going to have to expend a good bit of energy getting us there. For now it hadn't attacked anyone; what local authorities were left wereclearing out the area.

We all got ready as quickly as possible. Fortunately, Jamison had already showered and shaved; Zoe played with her long pixie-cut hair. I hadn't shaved in a month, or cut my hair in a year. Zoe had to remind me to shower last week.

Part of our Trinity edict was the dress code. Professional, yet tactical. Each of us wore black dress pants, but with steel-toe boots. I wore a basic white shirt and black tie, along with black suit coat. Of course, I also carried my katana, two guns and a clip belt. Zoe usually wore a white shirt, along with her red trench coat and black satchel. As our close quarters combat specialist, Jamison never wore a tie, but always wore a black vest. His shirts were often some ridiculous color, like today's pale purple.

Okay, we did look pretty badass.

"You got a photo of where we're going?" asked Zoe.

I showed her the picture on my phone. She stared at it for almost a minute, committing it to memory. Then she nodded, and took both our hands. Closing her eyes, she began to mumble words, a mantra of her own making. Concentric circles formed around us and began to spin, circles upon those circles. Blue energy cascaded up from the floor and crackled as it touched us. Her words were in the energy, and the words had power. The room faded from view as the light grew brighter. I shut my eyes and squeezed Zoe's hand as reality snapped.

"What the fuck!"

I opened my eyes to see we had arrived at the place the picture was taken – and vaporized the front end of a police car.

A cop came roaring forward. "You! Stop right there."

In a single motion, Jamison swung his arm and summoned a battle axe an inch away from the cop's face. "Trinity Unit Forty-Three. We were going to go kill a Wight, but if you want to play fiddle-dicks, we can jet."

A clusterfuck right off the bat.

"Jamison, put that away," I said, before turning to the cop. "Officer, please alert your CO that we've arrived."

The cop sputtered into his radio while my teammate waved away his weapon with a shrug. A few more cops had tentatively gathered around, hands on their guns. Some loved us and the help we provided, some found us just as terrifying as the Wights. Right now, I had other concerns.

"You okay?" I asked Zoe.

"Yeah, just a little drained," she said, popping a few vitamins and guzzling back a bottle of water. "I should be fine."

"Well, here comes the lieutenant. This jurisdictional pissing contest should be over soonish. Let me know if you need more time."

AFTER I HAD OFFERED a few calming words, while Jamison gazed threateningly behind me, everything had been smoothed over. We left the perimeter and headed off towards the parking garage. Zoe was already doing much better, so I felt like we were on top of this.

There weren't many vehicles inside from what we understood – people simply no longer coming into the city with the

Wight threat looming. We weren't sure if there was anyone inside, but initial assessments determined it was empty. That was the good news. The bad news was that power had been cut to the building somehow. The authorities didn't seem to know what had caused it, but all we'd have were a few windows and emergency lights by the exits.

Standing by the entrance, I clicked my tongue and considered the best strategy. There were a number of options. Kneeling down, I put one hand to the ground and the other to the side of the building. The parking garage was too big for my ability to fully map out, but I got the general layout.

"Hey, you guys want flashlights?" asked Jamison, summoning two of them.

Zoe made a sphere of green light the size of soft ball appear. "Nah, I got this. It's offense, too. Thanks, though!"

"I didn't know you had flashlights in your arsenal," I said, taking one. "That's convenient."

Jamison nodded and pulled a large hand gun out of the aether. "I toss all kinds of stuff in there. Anything I think might be useful, not just weapons. Change of clothes, phone charger, snacks, blankets, whatever."

Zoe began cackling. "It's a purse! It's your fucking purse."

"Yeah, I'm going to drop your skinny ass in my fucking purse."

"I'm all aflutter at that comeback, really."

I worked with children. "Can we go kill a Wight now?"

The three of us slipped into the garage, Zoe taking point with her glowing ball. It's greenish cast made everything look more eerie than it needed to, but I didn't say anything. The others didn't seem bothered by it. We cleared the ground floor, checking around each vehicle, inspecting every shadow. The place was silent, utterly still.

We found the stairs, one of the only sections still illuminated. Nothing here, no signs of activity of any kind. On the third floor we continued in the same fashion. There were even less vehicles up here that we could make out, perhaps only a dozen. They were all sedans or small SUV's, with a couple of trucks. Examining all of them, I began to wonder about this mission.

Wights could appear virtually anywhere, a loving home and a busy highway, or a cornfield and an abandoned factory. There was no pattern or reason, but it almost all circumstances, they began to wreak havoc. A Wight didn't lay low or stalk its prey. It could take all manner of forms, even humanoid, but it was little more than a savage beast.

With the second floor cleared, we moved to the third. This garage only had four floors, so we knew we were closing in. Every inch was swept over, weapons at the ready. I could hear Jamison grumbling, beginning to lose his cool. He held his gun in his right and balanced on his left wrist, his left hand holding the flashlight; he hadn't expected this to take so long. Whether it was nerves or impatience, I was ready to tackle this as well.

"Zoe, are you picking up anything?" I asked.

I could immediately tell something was wrong. She looked confused, possibly ill. She was sweating and the corners of her mouth were pulled back in a grimace.

"Zoe? You okay?"

"Everything is… off."

She and I had the opposite abilities in many ways. Everything came down to the wielding of Gias in some form. For instance, Jamison could create a pocket dimension he called his "arsenal," filled with weapons and whatever else he needed at will. I instinctively understood Gias and how that energy interacted in everything, while Zoe had the ability to manipulate Gias in a variety of raw states. In many ways, she was the most powerful of us.

"What the hell do you mean?" asked Jamison.

Zoe didn't say anything, but instead continued marching forward. We kept up behind her, trying to clear the floor, but she no longer appeared concerned with that. Instead, she hit the stairs, nearly running up them. We followed, exchanging a look. She burst out onto the final floor, the two of us right behind her, but nothing sprang out. It was just as desolate as the previous floors.

Zoe was muttering to herself. "I don't get it. I can still taste it."

I came up next to her. "What are you talking about?"

"It's nothing, I was wrong," she said.

We swept the floor, finding nothing as we had with the rest of the parking garage. It was possible the Wight had fled, moved on to some other part of the city, but I had a hard time believing that. I couldn't fathom the perimeter composed of local authorities were that incompetent. Jamison kept bitching we had been called out on a false alarm, but Zoe's reaction told me a different story. As we descended to the third, I decided to do one more scan of the building once we reached the center of that floor.

About a dozen paces out onto the third floor, I heard a high-pitched giggling. I spun, unable to determine were it was coming from. Jamison had done the same, but Zoe had gone as still as a statue.

"Little meat, little meat, how many cuts to make you bleat?"

The voice was like a little girl's, but somehow gravelly, a sound so perverse that I felt disturb the flow of Gias to my fingertips. My flashlight dipped for a moment as I shook off its effects. Another round of giggles.

I could hear Jamison swearing behind me. "What the sloppy fuck is that?"

"Sloppy? Sloppy-boppy? Like when we carve new holes in you to explore, to violate? Bibitty-Bobitty fuck! Little meat will squeal because that's what little meat does."

I watched as *it* strolled casually out of the shadows. It was as fully formed as a large human man, obsidian black, with unruly hair and one bright white eye that glowed with malevolent intent. It ran its hand up and down its chest in a sensual manner before reaching down and stroking its erection.

The Wight didn't look like this, the Wight didn't talk. This was something wholly new and terrifying.

It did something like a little dance. "When the…"

Jamison opened fire. He had swapped out his handgun for an assault rifle when I wasn't looking. He riddled the sinuous thing before with bullets and it collapsed on the ground.

Seconds later, another stepped out, absorbing the carcass of the first into itself.

"Stomp your feet and gnash your teeth!" it said, voice full of glee. "Such bold little beasts, full of vigor and bleach. Bleach? That's not the right word. Oh well."

I took a step forward. "What are you?"

"Your great answer from beyond the Deeper Black, one of the majestic State Entropic. We have so many names, one grand purpose. And all fall, fall, fall before the Everending. Isn't that right cousin? Shall we kiss and make it proper?"

At this point I was more than slightly confused.

Then Zoe burst into bluish-green flame of pure Gias energy.

"Here, try not to choke on your fascist bullshit."

A deluge of liquid flame erupted from her, flooding the entire parking garage. The Wight giggled as it was engulfed, and I covered my head, only to find the fire completely missing me. Utterly surrounded, I felt the heat, but wasn't singed a bit. The impossible magic only lasted ten seconds, but it felt like hours as the waves basted the concrete multistory.

The flames died, and we all stood there, everything as it had been. The Wight was gone.

"How did you do that?" asked Jamison.

"Fuck you, that's how."

I gently touched her elbow. "Zoe, please."

She stared at the ceiling, rubbing her temples. "Fine, let's go home."

Without touching us or using any incantations, she teleported us back.

Jamison sat on the couch with a drink. "What do you think?"

I shrugged. "She stole one of your bottles of moonshine and took it into the shower with her. That sounds like a normal Tuesday for Zoe."

"You can't be serious?"

"No, I'm not. But I'm prepared to hear her out."

"I mean, I love that dizzy bitch like a sister. I'd never tell her that, but it's true. I don't want to think that she's behind this in some way."

"I think I'm actually going to need some of that booze," I said, getting up and going for a cup.

"Why is everyone drinking my hooch?"

"Because it could strip paint off a deck," said Zoe, walking in and still drying off her hair.

She had changed into skimpy gym shorts and a baggy tee shirt. I tried not to look at her legs. She really was attractive, but I had always pushed that to the back of my mind because it felt unprofessional. Given the current circumstances, now it just made me sad.

"Could you make me a drink, too?" she asked.

"You need to be wasted for this conversation?" asked Jamison.

"I need to be hammered to process the knowledge you love me like a sister. I'm so touched!"

"How the raw fuck did you hear that?"

Zoe laughed. "If I wanted, I can hear things happening in London right now."

Jamison sat back on the couch. "Well shit, Zoe."

I brought her the drink she had requested and sat next to her. "Maybe you should start at the beginning."

"That could be… difficult. Let's start with the Wight Invasion. You all think it's a supernatural event, but it's not. It's an invasion, but it's from outside forces."

"Like aliens?" asked Jamison.

"Kind of. You'd be so lucky if it was just another race of sentient life forms. No, there are greater races out in the cosmos, sometimes called Houses or Pantheons. They're what you consider gods. They don't necessarily have physical bodies, although they are confined by the laws of physics most of the time. It's complicated."

I had so many questions, I didn't know where to start.

Jamison did though. "So evil alien gods want to destroy the earth? Awesome."

"They're not 'evil,' per se. Morality as you understand it doesn't apply to them. This particular House is, well, a death congregation. More than death, They're one of the Entropics. They embody extinction and ruin, often referred to as the Everending."

"That still sounds pretty uncool to me. That Wight we met was the definition of a cocksmack."

"Yeah, he's simply known as The Voice of The End. Looks like he's picked up some adorable new personality traits from his time on earth."

I stared at my cup. "How do you know that? How do you know any of this?"

Zoe sighed. "There are other Houses, too many to count. Powerful and old. They don't usually bother in cosmic affairs, it's considered unseemly. However, there's been more, uh, *activity* in recent years. Those from outside have stepped in, so we've stepped up."

Jamison and I stared at her. I tried to wrap my head around her words, what she was saying to me. The idea that the young woman drinking moonshine out of a plastic mug and wearing a shirt with a cartoon moose on it was in fact divinity.

Zoe burst out laughing. "Matsuda, you look like a puppy beat with a sack of rocks."

"I'm coming to terms with this!"

"Meanwhile, I'm regretting a whole lot of the shit-talk I've thrown your way," said Jamison.

"Don't you dare," she said. "I fucking adore you two. I never told either of you, because I loved just being a normal person by your side. I'm heavily depowered in a human form, but I'm still way stronger than I let on. I did that so I could hang out with you, be your friend. That doesn't mean I wasn't doing all I could to stop the threat of the Everending. I won't stop now, but I would love keep doing it next to you two jackoffs."

"I have always been honored to fight by your side," I said taking her hand. "That hasn't changed."

"I have one question," said Jamison.

"Just one?"

"No, but the first of many."

"For fuck's sake, okay."

"What's your real form look like?"

"So like, picture a supernova, right?"

"Right?"

"Yeah, nothing like that."

THE CONVERSATION WENT on for many more hours. Zoe told us what she could. She said some information couldn't properly translate into that which humans could understand, and while I accepted that, I still got the impression she was holding back. There was no reason to push her on it at this point, but it had me wondering.

As Jamison and I now understood it, the Everending had

discovered earth and found all the life forms here appalling. The very idea of propagation itself was utterly anathematic to them. From what Zoe had deduced, the Everending had dropped down into various points of natural Gias and festered, corrupting the energy. Once it had built up enough entropic energy, it lashed out at any nearby life form, infecting it and turning it into a what we knew as a Wight.

This was huge. I wanted to take all this to the higher ups, but Zoe asked me to hold back. She had seen enough of humanity to know that such upper brass either wouldn't believe me or simply view her as an enemy combatant. Reluctantly, I was forced to agree.

More had been said and plans had been made, and while the other two had retired for the night, I couldn't sleep. It wasn't the Zoe's revelations that kept me up, but the fact we had our hands tied. Eating yet another piece of cold pizza, I fumed over the whole affair.

The world was in turmoil over the Wight Invasion. Everything had come to a grinding halt, economies in collapse, countries starving, half a billion dead across the globe. We hadn't seen anything this bad since the Covid pandemic years ago. Just like then, America had corrupt politicians in charge that downplayed the severity to further their own ends.

The current administration was lead by a fundamentalist lunatic, President Charles Aster, who was unfortunately also terribly charismatic. The only reason he hadn't tried to defund the Trinity Units was because one had saved his daughter early on in his campaign. Aster might view the "demonic Wights" as a great threat, but he did see us a Holy Warriors, or some nonsense. Sadly, although his child's rescue was God's will, anyone else who died at the hands of a Wight was obviously a filthy sinner. His god would only send the Trinity Units to save the righteous, it would seem.

That same twisted mentality applied to rest of the country. If you couldn't help yourself, you deserved no help from

Washington. Aster vetoed every aid and stimulus bill, nixed every bail out and new tax plan. Instead, every oppressive law he tried to force through was intended to strip away rights and bring about a theocracy.

He wasn't very popular, except with a certain demographic.

The problem was, in this modern America, it was easy to say the Wights were demons, but selling Zoe as a benevolent deity would be nearly impossible. My upper brass might accept it, but when it got to the top, there'd be a shit-storm. No, this was up to us.

I MADE my way out into the main section of the warehouse to find Jamison laying on a weight bench. Sweat poured off of him, and he'd draped his forearm over his face.

"You good?" I asked.

"Definitely drank too much last night," he replied.

Zoe sauntered in with some pills. "Doctor Zoe prescribes rest, water, two ibuprofen, and to never try matching me drink for drink again. I'll put it in a sippy cup for you next time."

Jamison laughed under his arm. "Ah yes, I wondered when the verbal abuse would start."

I ran my fingers through my hair. "Are you going to be okay?"

"Shower then coffee. Yeah, I'll be fine."

As Jamison walked away, Zoe yelled after him. "Wait, did you want that coffee in a sippy cup then? You weren't clear!"

Jamison threw up a middle finger. "Fuck off, ya divine cunt."

"There's so much love and support there," said Zoe, hands to her heart.

As EXPECTED, another call came in not far from the previous one. Zoe suspected now that The Voice had made contact, it would want to continue what it had started. The worrisome part was the human-like traits it had displayed. She had said the Everending wasn't intrinsically evil, but The Voice had presented itself in a sadistic way. Given it was in a human form, I had to wonder about the man it was using as a vessel.

Jamison and I were getting ready as Zoe strolled in eating a bag of chips. I didn't remember us ever picking up chips, nor the soda she pulled out of the refrigerator. It was clear that Jamison had noticed all this, too.

"You going to get dressed, or are you going to keep eating food you had stashed away?"

Zoe waved her hand. For a split second she wasn't completely corporeal, then rendered fully again, dressed in her usual attire. Energy crackled in her hand, a small box appearing. She held it out to Jamison.

"What's this?" he asked.

"Open it."

Inside were four hot wings with a side of bleu cheese dressing.

Her hand crackled again. This time a held a plate with four pieces of sushi. California roll. She handed it to me. It looked just like the kind I used to get back when I was a detective out west.

"We have a few minutes," she said.

"Damn, girl," said Jamison.

I picked up a piece of sushi. "I worry this could be ominous."

"Shut up and eat."

THE BUILDING WAS LARGE, fifty-six floors. Multiple sightings, but reports were disjointed. We didn't know if it was one Wight moving throughout the floors or we had various targets. It didn't help that we were dealing with a few hundred entitled corporate types who felt we needed to deal with this immediately so they could get back to their greed.

"I have bad news and worse news," said Zoe, as they walked through the front doors.

"I'd expect nothing less," I said. "Hit me."

"There's easily two dozen humans still in this building. Maybe more. I can't really tell where with all the Entropic energy washing over me."

"Was that the worse news?"

"Oh no! The worse news is that there's something like eight Wights in here along with The Voice. We're right fucked."

Jamison pulled a shotgun out of his arsenal. "Your optimism is infectious."

I knelt down and touched the ground. The building was far too big to get any kind of proper reading on, but I could attempt it every few floors. My abilities surged out and I got a decent take on the first three floors. Nothing. Zoe confirmed my analysis as best she could. Nothing appeared damaged or even out of place, but we still choose to take the stairs over the elevator.

Though the stairwell was bright and clean, I still felt a sense of impending doom I had't been able to shake since the carpark. We slunk up, waiting for hell to rain down upon us. No such thing happened. We continued in this fashion, stopping every three floors for Zoe and I to try and get some basic read.

We found no people or Wight activity until we reached the twelfth floor. Now, I could feel something above, but it was hard to make out. Usually I could deduce just about anything using my powers, but this time there were conflicting probabilities, variables that didn't equal out. It was a board room, that much I knew, but after that it went off. Multiple but individual. People, alive but also dead. Not Wight, but there was Everending energy. This wasn't The Voice, this wasn't anything, but it was there. I pulled back as a headache began to blitz at the back of my skull.

I did my best to explain all of this to the others. Jamison looked skeptical, and Zoe said she could only feel Everending energy at this point. Seeing me rub my head, she materialized more pain pills and a bottle of water. I had to laugh at that satchel being a cover for her immense power all this time.

We reached the fourteenth floor. Whatever I had felt had been here. We fanned out, each going down a hallway. It was a typical office setting, lots of cubicles, computers, and coffee mugs. I couldn't even tell what went on here, it was so drab and lifeless. This could have been anything from a law firm or financing, to marketing or telecommunications. More CEOs who thought their little corner of the world were somehow essential, one percenters who horded their wealth while the world was torn apart by monsters. I buried my rage and concentrated on the mission.

I kicked in a couple doors, but found nothing. Growing frustrated, I was about to double back when Jamison called out. Bolting down the hall, I rounded the corner to find him standing outside one of the boardrooms.

It was bad. I don't think there was any way to determine how many people had once been in the room. Given the general mass of viscera and blood quantity, I'd say eight. Maybe seven, I don't know. It was like they had been put in a blender.

"I mean," said Jamison. "Could there be *more* blood everywhere? Jesus, what do you even say to something like this?"

Zoe came down to us, wearing a frown. She opened her mouth to say something, then peered into the room. Her original words died, replaced by a cry,

"It's a bomb!"

As the scene before me began to shimmer, I saw the carnage grow black and bubble with eldritch energy. Even as we appeared in the lobby downstairs, the force of the Entropic explosion hurled us across the room. The building shook, as windows shattered and fragments of the ceiling fell loose.

I glanced over at Jamison. He seemed fine, but Zoe staggered as she tried to stand. Whatever had hit us seemed especially lethal to her. I moved towards her, but before I could get near, entire portions of the building began to break away.

The ceiling was torn asunder, ripped open like a wound, with stray debris around its jagged edges and leaking water instead of blood. It was impossible to see how far it went up, but I would've guessed about fourteen storys. From the hole climbed a massive Wight composed of those mutilated bodies; it was a midnight colored beast the size of a tank, something like a lobster with a canine head.

"I thought it blew up?" said Jamison.

Zoe brushed her bangs out from her eyes. "It did."

Then the giggles started.

"Feeble flesh is feeble! But it does indeed have it uses."

We all turned to see The Voice standing behind the receptionist desk, scribbling on a piece of paper with a pen. He held up a childlike drawing of three severed head complete with Xs for eyes and what must have been himself standing behind triumphant. Highly amused, he started on his next masterpiece.

Zoe briefly closed her eyes. "I don't feel any more humans in this building. There's nothing but the Everending now."

I gave her a look. "You mean The Voice…"

"Yeah."

"Fine," said Jamison. "We don't have to hold back."

He swung his arms, swapping his shotgun out for a rocket launcher. In a single motion, he went to a knee and fired at the monster coming from the ceiling. The explosion rocked the already unsteady building, gaining a roar from the beast.

Before I could ask, a belt of grenades were tossed my way. I tapped in and tried to gauge its weaknesses. As I suspected, anything under its belly. I dodged to the left as Jamison continued a frontal assault, keeping it occupied. Zoe stormed off to confront The Voice.

Instead of taking the time to reload his RPG after every shot, Jamison simply threw it back into his arsenal and grabbed a new, loaded one. It made me wonder how many of those things he had ready. He'd already fired off six volleys. I'd gotten close enough to pitch a grenade underneath the creature, but it hadn't been close enough. I was, however, able to get a better read on its more sensitive areas: The center of what might be the thorax.

Weaving between a few chairs, I had to hit the deck when a giant claw tore through the front of the building, raining glass down everywhere. We were going to have to bring an end to this soon before the place came down on our heads. Sliding closer, I motioned to Jamison to shoot near its back. He nodded and took aim. Just as the rocket hit, I hurled two grenades underneath it while it was laying low.

That did it. The stomach erupted into formless shadows, one of the claws losing shape. Another rocket and two more grenades later, and you could barely tell what it had been once. Jamison had switched back to the shotgun, pumping rounds into its face. I was heading to him when I saw Zoe.

Everything stopped.

Guns up, I sprinted madly across the lobby, firing everything at The Voice. I heard Jamison screaming behind me, but I didn't care. The Voice said something, but I didn't hear it either. Run. Shoot. Save. Kill.

Then the Everending were everywhere. Hundreds of them. Monsters of every shape and size. I fought, knowing I was going to die.

But I didn't.

Jamison pulled out some ridiculous weapon, and got us out of there. Just he and I. We broke into a coffee shop that I suppose had shut down because of the invasion. Injured and demoralized, we collapsed inside. Neither of us had enough extra Gias to heal ourselves, and now, no way to get home. What I had seen happen to Zoe was horrific. I lay there swaying back and forth between grief and rage.

Between death and vengeance.

It took days to gather our strength back. In that time, we made do with what little stock had been left behind, mostly bottle drinks and prepackaged cookies. Jamison did have those snacks in his arsenal, but I worried about maxing all those out when we had food at out disposal. While we rested, we took in the news.

Wight activity had increased tenfold across the planet the last three days, the Everending making their big move. They had every intention of cleansing the planet of life.

In perhaps the most insane moment in a week of insanity, came the news of President Aster's new Wight proclamation. The Voice, perhaps realizing that Aster was an anti-life shitbag at his core, convinced the deranged official that it was some kind of holy being. I believe "Sword of God" was the phrase being used by an American President to describe an alien invader bent on our termination. The Voice was now wandering around the White House, eating the remaining loyal staff members. Not that there were many left.

Trinity Units had been outlawed and many had been arrested. They'd use terms like domestic terrorist or national security threat to incarcerate anyone with enhanced Gias abilities so the Wights had free reign. Not that it would take long.

Jamison wanted to head out, take the fight to them. He

was definitely the type to mourn his friend by cracking skulls in her honor. Even if I could get behind that, neither of us were one hundred percent yet. Hell, we were barely at seventy.

Honestly, I didn't know what to do, even with my powers.

It was almost noon on the fourth day when I had opened a stale biscotti. Jamison was doing pushups and discussing options on how best to replenish his arsenal. I was only half paying attention when there was a burst of bluish-green light in the center of the room. I scrambled for my gun until I heard her voice.

"What's up, douchebags? Hey, is that a biscotti?"

Zoe stood there, utterly unharmed. More than that, she glowed with energy, radiating some type of higher power. Tiny bolts of lightning crackled from her eyes and off her body. Her ratty old red trench coat looked brand new, but also now had a black satin trim in gold filigree. The white shirt actually fit her and didn't have an ever-present food stain. Instead of steel-toed shoes, she now wore armored boots and her black pants looked woven out of something entirely unnatural. Her already attractive features looked somehow flawless now.

Yeah, *this* Zoe was divine.

"Okay, yeah, you're lookin' like a smoke show, but what the fuck, girl?" said Jaimson.

"And you look remarkably like a flaccid penis," said Zoe. "What's the problem here?"

I may have lost it. "I saw you die! You were… in pieces!"

Zoe's lightshow abruptly stopped as her eyes went wide. "Shit, you actually thought I was dead?"

"Pieces! And those pieces were…"

Zoe knelt down in front of me and pulled me into a hug. "Matsuda, this isn't my real body. It's a proxy that I cram about thirty percent of my essence down into. Either The

Voice didn't realize that or it didn't care. Regardless, I thought *you* guys understood that!"

"We did not," I said, hugging her back.

"He was very sad," said Jamison, sniffing. "One morose little bitch."

Zoe reached out an arm. "Shut up and come here, you cuddly fuckwad."

The three of us hugged, and for a moment, things felt better. Then reality set back in.

"Things have gotten way worse since you left," I said. "Our lunatic president has decided The Voice is an angel of the Lord. It's going to be a very stupid apocalypse."

"Damn it. I would have been here sooner, but I needed to gather up celestial energies that could be malleable out of the dark flow. For you two I've been gone for days, but for me it's been a few centuries."

"Oh. Uh, thank you?"

"What do you need, eh, whatever for?" asked Jamison.

Zoe materialized the cigarette looking box she had used to stuff defeated Wights into. I realized she no longer had her satchel.

"What exactly is that thing?"

"It's just a depository. It's honestly bullshit. I just needed something to make you guys believe I was human. Before, I'd drop Wights into it and then instantly zap them off to the far side of the universe. This time however, I carried something back."

She opened the lid to reveal two orbs the size of marbles, emanating such raw, unrestrained power that I fell back to the floor. They were the same color as the energy Zoe used, but I felt as If I was staring at a preternatural phenomena. Something cosmic.

All I could do was whisper. "What are those?"

"Remember a while back when you were tossing theories around about Gias and Wights? You wondered which came first? Well, the Wights came first. The Everending showed up and began perverting earth life forms to bring about its extinction. That pissed me off, so I showed up and flicked one of these into the human Gias field. I'm the one that advanced it with celestial technology."

Jamison laughed. "So you're shoving two more in?"

"Oh, hell no! I'm shoving one in each of you."

THAT WAS YESTERDAY. It took about a day to acclimate to what we had become. We're not as powerful as Zoe, but neither of us are human any longer. Teleportation, instant regeneration, low levels of telekinetics, and telepathy among the three of us. Most importantly, our specialized abilities.

Jamison can now create an arsenal approximately half the size of the planet. Anything from anywhere can be summoned in and out of it, as long as he knows where it's at. Before it was just a void, but now he's been able to turn it into a sort of livable habitant. I no longer have limits on my situational awareness. All things, everywhere, are constantly calculated and mapped out. Everything is part of the pattern now.

We have a plan.

I've sent this out to all social streams and news nets, dated for twelve hours after our attack. My enhanced abilities allowed me to easily hack everywhere. Even if we don't succeed in freeing the earth, the truth will be free. None of us expect to survive this, even in our enhanced states.

The Voice is at the White House, along with Aster and a large contingency of Wights. There, I plan to locate every Wight on the planet, and through our telepathic link, have Jamison summon them into his arsenal. Every single one of them, including The Voice, Aster, and any human loyal to the Everending. Then the three of us will step in and end this.

When we were preparing, Zoe had made the joke, "Death is a serious medical condition."

Jamison had laughed. "In the twenty-first century, so is life."

Typical banter, but it stayed with me as I wrote all this down. We cling to life because we believe we deserve it, but the Everending feel they are just as much in the right. *We're* the abomination to them.

I used to considered myself a moral relativist for the most part, but some ideals are simply wrong. You can't be neutral in the face of an ideology that glorifies genocide and oppression. It may seem hyperbole in these times, but some things are just evil.

That's why we're going, because it's the right thing to do.

Our names were Zoe, Jamison, and Matsuda. I hope we don't fail you.

OUROBOROS MORNING

THE WORLD IS GOING to end today. That's okay, it ends every day.

Ted is killing his wife again. He does that most days. I have no idea why she just doesn't leave after the reset each time. I suppose she has nowhere to go. Getting stabbed on my front lawn every other afternoon doesn't sound like fun. From the look on Ted's face, he's not even enjoying it anymore.

The neighbors used to try and intervene. Nobody bothers anymore.

Away from the curtain, I go back to the kitchen table to pick at my meal. The same selection of food I've had for one thousand, seven hundred and twelve days. Granted, I've gone out a handful of times, but that usually ends badly. People were brutal that first year. Most have calmed down and settled into this cyclical nightmare, but I'm not willing to risk it anymore.

Today it was tuna fish and cheese slices on crackers. I hate tuna fish, it was one of those things Neil ate. You learn to make do when your options are limited. It doesn't hurt when you wash it down with a bottle of red.

I've read every book in my house twice, and borrowed

some off the neighbors. I tried to take up a few hobbies like crocheting, but any progress I make gets reset the next day. Most days I down all the alcohol in the house and pass out early.

Water and gas work most of the time, but electricity is spotty. Communication services went down almost immediately. I assume most people aren't going to work anymore, I don't know. Utilities won't run themselves indefinitely, even on a loop.

Honestly, all I want is my phone. I want to talk to Neil. I haven't spoken to my husband in over four years now. Away in Boston on a business trip, there's no way he can make it home before the reset. Hell, I'd be willing to brave the outside to find him, but I'm not sure where he could even be in that city. I've never been to Boston.

I know he's still alive. Even if he *has* died, he'll come back. I've died thirty-six times, and I wake up again every morning in the same ratty Misfits tee-shirt.

We all live in that Bill Murray movie, but the horror version.

Most of my lunch goes in the trash. I haven't been eating much and have dropped weight. Usually I'd be happy about that, but can't find the enthusiasm to care. I've found the word "melancholy" best describes my state of being. That sounds better than "depressed apathy".

Moving through this house like a ghost, filling it with pointless actions that lead to nothing. Going through the motions of a life, preprogramed to look something like a human. At this point, there is only blank acceptance.

Everyday is sunny here, but I'm only in the shadows.

The notion of actually getting dressed faded long ago. I wear the same underwear and Misfit tee I slept in all day, every day. They're always clean after the reset. Grabbing a second bottle of wine, I make for the back porch. Our yard out back is small, but pretty. Vines climb up the short wooden fence and bloom into bright purple flowers. Tending the garden is pointless. We have a large, cement birdbath and Neil's precious grill pushed just out from under the awning.

I recline in one of the chairs, leg up, unconcerned about my half-naked state. I've seen far worse out there. People butchered, sold, even eaten. While all these atrocities still occur, a lot of it has dropped off. My theory is, once people realized none of it mattered, that everything returned to the status quo the following day, interest was lost in a short time. It was like video games: you grew bored playing the same level over and over if there was no lasting impact, no progress to the next arena.

I got it. During all this, I had killed eleven people myself. I had almost vomited after my first, stricken with regret, even though he had tried to rape me. By the eleventh, it was just an annoyance.

The butterflies come out and flitter around the flowering vines. One of those tiny bright moments of the day that makes me smile. From what I've heard, animals are as free as us, so it makes me happy that the butterflies come back each afternoon. They are my only friends. That sounds so pathetic, but I pushed away the few other people I was close with in the area. It was too dangerous, too detrimental.

I wassleeping with the kid from a few houses down for a while. Aiden. Maybe three months? He was back from college for the summer, which was good or bad depending on your point of view. At thirty, I'm a decade older than him, which he didn't seem to mind at all. I could give all kinds of reasons why I did it, but ultimately, I simply wanted to feel something good. It got broke off when it no longer began to feel that way.

That about six months ago now. It's so hard to keep track. It's hard enough to keep count of the days, but I'm determined.

Sometimes I think about getting ahold of Aiden. To just

talk or get him naked, either one. This loneliness is grinding my bones, turning me to dust. But the guilt is worse, hollowing me out in a way that's more painful. Worse of all, it all keeps twisting inside of me and turning into resentment.

Fuck Neil for going to Boston and leaving me alone in this.

After a few hours of porch drinking, I usually eat a little something else and then dive into the harder stuff. My big decision of the day is always between gin and vodka, along with the occasional wild contender of tequila. We were well stocked before the loop started, and I'd normally be hammered by eight o'clock, passed out by ten. As always, I wake up to a new day at eight am.

It is still a little early, only four, but I hadn't eaten much at lunch and I had to pee. Sitting on the toilet, I consider what to make. Nothing sounds good, per usual. Finishing up, I exit the bathroom and proceed into the kitchen. Glancing towards the living room, I see a commotion out front on the street.

I know I should ignore it, but I can't.

It's a group of people, six or seven. All of them are wearing black robes except for one, a man dressed in all white with long white hair. He doesn't look old, though. He's young and handsome.

The Man in White seems to be some type of preacher, although I can only make out part of what he was saying. A number of my neighbors have come out to hear his sermon, and it's obvious they don't like what he is saying. I crack the door and peek out, trying to get a better gist of what is going on.

"… not an accident or a cosmic mistake," he said. "We are embraced by the divine, held in purposeful cycle."

"What fecking purpose?" says Ted, shaking the same garden shears he's just used to kill his wife.

"Who are we to know the machinations of gods? Yet we are bound by celestial wonder and you too may bare witness to its glory."

Aiden's mom starts screaming. She doesn't like me much and I get the impression she screams a lot. I also get the impression she makes me look sober.

"That's devil talk!" she screeches. "This is a good neighborhood and we don't want your kind here!"

Hysterical that she would say this about some weird preacher, but allow Ted to stand there and brandish gardening tools still wet with his wife's blood. I've always hated this neighborhood and its hypocrisy, but Neil loved the house. There was that resentment again.

The Man in White shakes his head. "Do you truly wish to remain blind? Willfully ignorant? We will leave, but you will forever be lost in yourselves."

A man from down the street lifts a sledgehammer. "You ain't leaving, pal. We gotta send a message. This neighborhood is protected."

It hits me that everyone from our neighborhood is armed. I can't believe I was so drunk I hadn't noticed. From what I can make out, it is a random assortment of weapons, with only a few handguns scattered among them. This was a pretty liberal state, and there wasn't a lot of hunting in this area. Still, this is about to go very badly for the religious folk.

"You don't want to do this," says The Man in White.

"Sure we do," says one on my neighbors.

"Kill the Satanist!" screams Aiden's mom.

The Man in White gives a slight gesture and his followers all pull large automatic weapons from beneath their black robes. Without any hesitation or warning, they open fire on the gathering. Bullets tear through all of them, dropping all the assembled. No one from the neighborhood gets off a single shot.

It is a massacre. I drop to my knees, horrified. They deserved it and would be back tomorrow, but that still didn't mean I enjoyed watching it. From the crack in the door, I can see blood draining out of Aiden's mouth. I hadn't even seen him among the crowd.

Pulling the door open slightly farther, I see The Man in White is staring right at me.

"Hello," he says.

I say nothing.

"You were not a part of this?"

"No, I had no idea. I was too drunk to… no."

He walks halfway up my sidewalk. "I'm sorry for this. Please tell them that."

"I don't really talk to anyone."

"I see."

We stare at each other.

He gives a little smile. "Do you wish to know?"

"Know what?"

"The truth."

What do you say to that? Sure, his people had just slaughtered my neighbors, but they were all assholes. Even if he killed me, I'd be back. There was nothing he could do that hadn't already happened. I could only go up at this point.

"Sure," I say. "What's your truth?"

"It's simple. More and more people are discovering it. It's the one thing you have to see for yourself to remember, the memory of being told will fade the next day. Do you understand?"

I do. The Man in White tells me what to do and leaves with his followers. I'm not sure if I believe him, but I know this is my only shot. I put the booze away and start making coffee.

To be honest, I almost don't make it. I hadn't stayed up all night since everything began. Hell, I hadn't stayed up all night since my early twenties. But what amounted to two pots of coffee helps, and I find myself out on the back porch curled up in a blanket as time counted down to the reset.

"Look to the sky, look to the rising sun at dawn when it comes," he said.

I had assumed that the reset was the same time for everyone. Five Fifty-two am EST on June twenty-first. But the way he explained it, that apparently wasn't the case. Everyone experienced it at their dawn. I'm not sure how that is possible.

Coffee in hand, I watch as the sun begins to peek up over the horizon. The light grows brighter, and I begin to allow despair to sneak in, thinking this has all been for nothing. Stars blink out and the night recedes.

Then, for a brief few moments, they shimmer into existence.

They are massive, perhaps the size of countries. It is hard to tell from this perspective. High above the planet, encircling us like the rings of Saturn. Individual entities with some features as recognizable as eyes and limbs, others so alien that they defy description. Each one is unique, each unlike anything ever seen on Earth. Each reaching out and clasping the god to each side, a great circle surrounding our little planet.

The sun rises higher and my eyes take it all in. My mind struggles to process the grandeur, the complexity. I had hoped for an answer, but I had not expected this. No one could have.

Reset.

I awake in my bed, another day.

The Man in White told me this would happen, but instead of anguish, I feel lighter. Free. For the first time I can remember, I don't go downstairs and immediately hit a bottle of wine. No, I get dressed.

I'm going to live.

ABOUT THE AUTHOR

Brian Fatah Steele has been writing various types of dark fiction for over fifteen years, from horror to urban fantasy and science fiction. Steele originally went to school for fine arts but finds himself far more fulfilled now by storytelling. His own titles include OUR CARRION HEARTS (Bloodshot Books), HUNGRY RAIN (Severed Press), CELESTIAL SEEPAGE (Alien Agenda Publishing), BLEED AWAY THE SKY (Bloodshot Books) and THERE IS DARKNESS IN EVERY ROOM (Sinister Grin Press), along with the self-published YOUR ARMS AROUND ENTROPY, BRUTAL STARLIGHT, FURTHER THAN FATE, and IN BLEED COUNTRY. His work has appeared in such anthologies as 4POCALYPSE, BLOOD TYPE, CTHULHU LIES DREAMING, DEATH'S REALM, THE IDOLATERS OF CTHULHU, and the Bram Stoker Award-nominated DARK VISIONS, VOL.1.

www.ingramcontent.com/pod-product-compliance
Lightning Source LLC
Chambersburg PA
CBHW021531150726
47990CB00006B/2192